NIIBING JIINGTAMOK

Powwow Summer

Nahanni Shingoose

James Lorimer & Company Ltd., Publishers
Toronto

James Lorimer & Company Ltd., Publishers acknowledges funding support from the Ontario Arts Council (OAC), an agency of the Government of Ontario. We acknowledge the support of the Canada Council for the Arts, which last year invested $153 million to bring the arts to Canadians throughout the country. This project has been made possible in part by the Government of Canada and with the support of Ontario Creates.

Cover design: Tyler Cleroux
Cover image: Shutterstock

Library and Archives Canada Cataloguing in Publication

Title: Powwow summer / Nahanni Shingoose.

Names: Shingoose, Nahanni, author.

Identifiers: Canadiana (print) 20190130911 | Canadiana (ebook) 20190130938 | ISBN 9781459414150 (softcover) | ISBN 9781459414167 (epub)

Classification: LCC PS8637.H5254 P69 2019 | DDC jC813/.6—dc23

Published by:
James Lorimer &
Company Ltd., Publishers
117 Peter Street, Suite 304
Toronto, ON, Canada
M5V 0M3
www.lorimer.ca

Distributed in Canada by:
Formac Lorimer Books
5502 Atlantic Street
Halifax, NS, Canada
B3H 1G4

Distributed in the US by:
Lerner Publisher Services
1251 Washington Ave. N.
Minneapolis, MN, USA
55401
www.lernerbooks.com

Printed and bound in Canada.

For my dear friend (and editor) Kat. Thank you for believing in me and making this story possible. You are truly an exceptional teacher.

For my family: Steve, Sage, Ziibii, Mom, Dad and Howard. Thank you for supporting me in everything I do.

For my dear friend Liz Osawamick, and to Dr. Shirley Williams: Gchi Miigwech for helping me with the translation of Anishnaabemowin.

NBAKWENDAN

PROLOGUE
I Remember

People have always had a hard time figuring out my heritage when they first meet me. "What are you?" they ask.

I'm slightly brown, with freckles. My long, thick, black hair hangs to my waist. My clothes are always a little snug. I spent years in the centre of the back row in class pictures, looking down at my classmates. My cheekbones are high, and my eyes are dark brown. This used to inspire the boys in grade five to skip past me while singing, "Her lips were pink, like a hound dog's dink, and her eyes were dog-shit brown!"

When I was ten years old, my mom and my teacher (who are both French) talked me into fancy shawl dancing at the school's talent show. "It will be fun," they said.

Powwow music echoed through the gym from a Chippewa Travellers CD my mom picked up at the Rama Powwow. I wore the new beaded moccasins and leggings my auntie had made me, which matched the beadwork hanging from my braids. A single eagle plume stood upright from the hair clip at the back of my head. My shawl and skirt shimmered in the light. The ribbons on my shawl seemed to hover in the air as I began.

I started out with a lot of energy. But by halfway through the song my chest felt tight. I started to feel a stabbing pain in my calves every time my feet hit the floor. I wasn't in great shape, and no one had taught me to warm up my muscles. But still I twirled in circles, holding my arms high with my elbows out. I repeated the same steps over and over, just moving my feet from side to side instead of doing any fancy foot work.

Finally the drumming and singing ended. I fumbled to a stop a few seconds after the last beat. I couldn't seem to land at the same time as the music ended. Since then I've learned how to listen to the song. Now I understand that 'four times through,' means the drummers sing the same 'chorus' four times. To my surprise, students and staff sat silent during the music. I had thought that people would stand, clapping and smiling. I was sure they would love watching me dance because it would be so beautiful, so unique. I mean, that's how the crowd responds at powwows.

After I finished, there was a pause. Then they clapped. I curtsied before I walked off the stage. Why did I do that? Who curtsies after a fancy shawl dance? I was happy with my performance. But I felt embarrassed, almost ashamed.

It wasn't until the next day that I heard what staff and students felt about my dancing. Most of the teachers told me how beautiful I looked. A few students weren't as kind. I was in the washroom, in a stall, and I heard two girls come in.

"Did you see that ESKIMO girl dancing in the gym yesterday? IT WAS SO BAD," one said.

The other girl giggled and agreed. "My mom said she is an Indian. She says Indians are mostly drunk people on welfare and they get everything for free."

"Yeah, that girl is probably drunk at school."

"Yeah, I bet she drinks Listerine and sniffs gasoline from a paper bag."

"She probably lives in a tipi."

"Yeah, with fish guts in her bed."

"Yeah, probably."

"Yes, fish guts for sure."

I wanted to know what an Eskimo, an Indian and a drunk person were. I didn't know what welfare was, and I wanted to know what things I got for free. I wanted to know who in my family drank mouthwash and sniffed gasoline from a bag. Wouldn't the bag get wet? My mom was French and a school teacher, and my stepdad, also white, was a car salesman. My real dad was Ojibwe and a musician. The only time I saw other Indigenous people was when I spent a couple of weeks every summer with him in Winnipeg. At ten years old, I had never knowingly seen a drunk person. I guess I didn't recognize the results of my mom's Friday night wine-o-thons with her sister. I also never thought about them being white, and that I wasn't. I just didn't.

I never stood up to the two girls in the washroom, even though I knew who they were. And the teasing just got worse from that point. My braids were pulled by kids in the halls. It happened so fast, I could never turn fast enough to tell who it was. I was shy and couldn't stick up for myself anyway. Boys would run past me, or dance around me, raising their hands to pat their mouths while they made trills and war cries. When I told my teachers, they would tell me that the boys teasing me probably meant they liked me. They said that's what boys do when they like girls, they tease them. But I didn't want to be liked by a boy at that age. Not if it meant them bullying me. Tormenting me.

I enjoyed going to powwows and dancing. But after that, it never felt the same. I felt like someone was looking at me, judging me, making fun of me. If I were to give my younger self advice now, eight years later, it would be to speak out. As I make my way into being an adult, I want to try to be the person I needed when I was younger. Because did I ever need someone.

JIIGBIIG

CHAPTER 1
On the Beach

River shook the bottle, opened the lid with her teeth and poured sunscreen into her palm. She rubbed her hands together and smeared the coconut-scented lotion over Josh's bare shoulders. She made little white hearts with her two fingers. She turned and did the same to his little sister Jasmine, who was seventeen, only a year younger than Josh.

"You get some hearts too, Jazz, since you're such a sweetheart," River said with a smile. River glanced to where Jazz was looking and saw three barely teen boys gawking at them. She tried to ignore them.

River's friend Charlotte plopped down in front of her and swept her hair to the side. River massaged the sunscreen onto Charlotte's back and down her pale arms. Then she stood up to spread the sunscreen on her own arms and legs. She tried not to get any on her bikini. Not that there was much bikini to get it on. She glanced up at the boys once more. This time she held their gaze. Their cheeks were red, and the towels on their laps looked a little too strategic. River smiled at the boys from her great age of almost eighteen as if to say, "Seriously, guys? Just be a kid while you still can."

"Are you going to the Canada Day parade and fireworks, Riv?" Jazz asked.

"Maybe. I was thinking I could be a real Indian princess in the parade. You know, I could get one of those awful polyester costumes that cover only, like, half your body. I could wave like royalty as I ride my horse bareback." River managed to deliver the sentence without smirking. She waved her hand with her fingers together, rigidly, from side to side.

"You're terrible, River!" roared Charlotte.

"You would totally steal the show, Riv!" Jazz said. "I think you should do it."

"It would add some sex appeal," said Josh. "That's for sure."

River's hand met Josh's arm with a slap. He fluttered his puppy dog eyes, trying to earn her forgiveness.

"So, Riv, Charlie, what are we doing this summer? This is OFFICIALLY the last summer before university . . . so it needs to be epic." Josh smiled with his eyes closed.

"My relatives are coming from France, so I have to stick around for a few weeks in July. But I'd love to go camping or something," Charlie replied.

"Ooh la-la, Charlie!" Jazz's French accent was less than perfect. "Yeah, I'm down for camping. Grundy Lake is really nice."

"Yeah I like Grundy too," added River. "My grandparents used to take us there when we were small."

"Grundy it is!" crowed Josh. "Jazz, are you bringing a boy-toy?"

"Josh, you're a dog. A big, fat, hairy, stinky and stupid D-O-G." Jazz's smile, unlike her words, showed how much she adored her big brother.

"Ouch! So harsh. Jazz," Josh whined. "That's why you don't have a boy-toy. Just saying." Josh tilted his head to the left, and smiled back.

River could tell that Jazz was rolling her eyes behind her sunglasses. Raised as an only child, she wondered what having such relentless brother-sister banter would be like. Probably it would get tired really fast.

"I'm going to my dad's in Winnipeg last week of July. I'm back middle of August, I think," said River. "We could go camping the last weekend in August before the long weekend. Before school starts. Would that work?"

She smiled at Josh's pout at the idea of her going away even for a couple of weeks.

"That sounds like it might work for me," Jazz said, scrolling through the calendar on her phone.

"Yeah, me too, probably," added Charlie. "It has to be before Frosh Week though. What you doin' at your dad's house this summer, Riv? You guys have plans?"

"Well, just hanging out with my nokomis. That means grandma in Ojibwe. And my cousins on my dad's side might come up from Minnesota. We're gonna go to the powwow on the rez."

Charlie raised her eyebrows. "Holy, that's awesome. Sounds like fun."

"Yeah, I'm excited about the powwow. I'll meet some distant relatives and eat a ton of bannock. My nokomis is going to help me finish my jingle dress, and I'm going to dance."

"Oh that's so awesome. I love that you're still connected to your culture, Riv." Jasmine smiled.

Josh nodded in agreement.

"Well, I guess I am, sort of. I'd like to learn more though. It's not the same as living on the rez. I feel a little disconnected from it all. It's weird, trying to live in two worlds."

"What do you mean?" Josh asked.

"I don't know how to explain it really. It's like . . . I feel, like, happy where I am, and in my life and stuff. But I always feel like I'm missing out. I don't know on what — cultural stuff or something. I just feel like something's always missing. When I'm at my dad's, I feel, like, really happy, and part of the culture. But then of course I miss my life here. It's hard to find a balance I guess."

"Yeah I get it," Jazz said. "When our parents got divorced, I always felt torn between two families. I mean, it's not exactly the same, but sort of similar."

Josh nodded in agreement again.

Charlie yelled from under her large sun hat. "Um, hellooo, too depressing! This was supposed to be a fun day at the beach. And you're talking about feelings and stuff. And divorce and stuff. I don't want to think about adulting until it's absolutely necessary. Once we become adults, our life as we currently know it is OVER!"

Josh looked over at River and shrugged his shoulders. River liked how Josh was good at navigating awkward situations by deflecting with humour. Or just flat out changing the subject. "So is anyone going to Brittany's party tomorrow night? Lotsa babes and booze I heard."

Charlie winced. "Well I like the babes part. But not the booze part. I really wish I could find a girl that doesn't drink at all."

"Me too," Josh said.

"What the heck! I don't drink at all!" River squealed and slapped at Josh. "Charlie, what about that girl you met on the campus tour a few weeks ago?"

"I dunno, she was too weird. I don't think she was like a *real lesbian*. She was just like a, *I wanna try it out and see if I like it before I go back to men*, kinda lesbian. Look, I have a friggin' taco tattoo on my wrist. If you don't like tacos, then go back to the hot dog cart already. I can't be someone's experiment."

River spit out her drink as laughter roared from her belly. "That is so friggin' hilarious! But really, does it have to be one or the other? Can't it be both?"

Charlie shrugged her shoulders.

River continued, "So all in favour of *not* going to Brittany's party, *don't* put up your hands." She was greeted by the sight of no hands in the air. "Okay, amazing. It's final. We can all come to my house again tomorrow night then. We can have a bonfire and roast marshmallows or whatever. Josh and I will be back from riding at about three o'clock. That gives us plenty of time to put the horses away and stuff."

"Sounds good," Josh said, as the girls nodded in agreement.

Charlie pressed shuffle on her phone and turned up the volume. The four of them basked in the sun until dusk.

CHAPTER 2

Love is Good

The boards on the old stairs creaked as River snuck down into the basement of the farmhouse where she lived. Josh was there sleeping. His back was to her as she cuddled up under the blankets. She breathed in his scent with her nose burrowed in the hollow at the back of his neck.

"Don't tease me, River . . ." Josh begged. He rolled over and wrapped his arms around her.

She kissed him on the forehead, "Then let's go, cowboy! It's nine o'clock. Half the day is over!" She whipped the blankets to the floor and leaped off the couch. She tossed him his Adidas track pants and smirked. "These will look FAB-U-LOUS with your cowboy boots."

Josh pulled the blankets back up over his head and groaned. "Uggh, okay, girl. Let's pack and go then." He pulled on the pants under the blankets, hopped up and snapped the elastic around his waist. "I already packed the water bottles, snacks and bug spray last night, and the lunch is in the fridge."

"Did you pack a feed bag for the horses? They can drink from the lake once we get to the bluff."

"Oh no, I forgot. We can grab them when we saddle up, eh?"

"For sure. I'll just bring a bag of oats and a few carrots for

13

them." River smiled, standing with hands on her hips. "Thanks for this, Josh. I know this isn't your favourite thing to do. But it's gonna be fun, I promise. Don't forget a blanket." She winked.

"A blanket? For what?" Josh's voice inched up higher.

"To sit *on*. You know, *for lunch*. And then if you're good, we'll see what else we can do with, or under, it." River's cheeks turned pink as she turned toward the stairs.

"You drive me crazy, girl." Josh grabbed her by the waist and pulled her close. He kissed her softly. He pulled a strand of her long brown hair from her eyes and placed it behind her ear. "How long is this ride, anyway?" He raised his eyebrows.

"About an hour each way. We should be there before noon for sure. Let's saddle up and get going. I'm so excited I can't even handle it!"

"Okay, let's do this."

"Okay, I just have to pee first. I'll be right out."

In the bathroom, River stared at herself in the mirror. She wished she could see herself the way Josh seemed to. She put the tiniest splash of scent behind her ear.

They rode for about an hour, talking and laughing, mostly about the things they used to do as little kids. Catching tree frogs and making tiny villages with twigs and moss. Playing in the creek behind the school and getting soaked almost every recess. Driving their teachers and parents crazy.

When they got to the meadow, they trotted around looking for the perfect spot to set up their picnic. They found a clearing under some trees where the grass wasn't too long, near the water. River tossed the blanket to Josh, gesturing for him to lay it under the tree in the shade.

After she tied the mares to the trees and hung their feed bags, River didn't waste any time. She ran over to Josh, stripping down to her bikini. When she got to the blanket, she pulled him close and kissed him. She desperately wanted to sleep with him. But she was still a virgin and felt like she needed to wait for the right time. Whenever that might be. She didn't just want it to be a sex-only relationship, even though they had been together for a long time. They fooled around a lot, but never went all the way. Josh never pressured her, and always stopped when she asked him to. She could see he was trying to be patient about the whole thing. But they had never really talked about it, and she didn't bring it up much.

"Soo . . . I was thinking, Josh," she whispered. Her back tingled as he grazed his fingers up and down her spine.

"Wait." He put his finger on her lips. "Before you say anything else, I want to tell you how hot you look in this bikini." He kissed her neck.

River smiled. "Well, maybe I'll have to bring this bikini to college for the first time we . . . you know. I'm sure it would look better on a dorm room floor," she teased. "And I'm so excited we both got into the same university. Trent is going to be awesome. We can finally do everything together. There's a river where we can go paddling. I hear there is lots of great music in the park . . . and there's a ton of . . ."

Josh stepped back, his hands still resting on her hips. "Are you serious, Riv? That's the plan, for us to have sex for the first time then? I mean, that's like three months away. You're gonna make me wait until after the summer is over?" His eyebrows were stern.

"Whoa . . . like . . . does it bother you? Having to wait?" Her smile faded.

"I'm an eighteen-year-old guy, Riv. I can't help it. I'm so in love with you. You've been my girl since like grade three." His hands were waving in the air, and then fell to his side. "I mean, I don't really mind. I just thought it would be sooner than that. Like maybe this summer. But if you want to wait, of course I'll wait."

"Okay, well, I want to wait."

They were both silent. His body was stiff. Hers was rigid.

"I thought a college dorm would be the perfect place. Then no one will be around to, like, interrupt us," River continued.

"All right. I can do that."

River could tell Josh was disappointed. But he still pecked her on the lips.

River turned away and the words spilled from her mouth. She tried to fill the silence between them with plans. "So wanna swim, and then have lunch? Then we can maybe go jump off the cliffs or something, and then head home? The girls are coming over after dinner. We need to pick up marshmallows for the campfire tonight on our way back." She knew she always talked really fast when she was nervous.

"Okay, sounds like a great plan." Josh smiled, but River could tell he was anything but happy.

River took his hand and led him to the water. Their bodies shivered as their toes met the sand. They played in the water, and on shore, as if they were eight years old again.

CHAPTER 3

The Women Set the Table

When they got back to the farm, River and Josh carried the tack inside the barn and dried the sweat off the horses with a towel. River's mom called them from the kitchen door, and they made their way up to the house.

River's forehead was beading with sweat. Her red bandana never seemed to keep it from dripping onto her brow. It became a cakey mess as dust was thrown up from the tires of her stepdad's truck. By the time he had sped up the long dirt driveway and skidded beside them, the dust was a waist-high cloud. River glared at Randy as he brought the truck to a stop.

Why speed up a driveway? she thought.

"I'm going in to freshen up," River said to Josh. She tried to avoid Randy's eye as she went inside and washed her hands at the kitchen sink. She scrubbed the dirt from under her fingernails. It was a habit River had had since her mom told her that, when she was small, they would get the strap at school if their fingernails were dirty. River figured it was a good habit for a farm girl to have.

"Are you staying for dinner, Josh?" River's mom asked.

"Thanks for the invite," he replied. "But I need to get home and clean up a bit. But I'll be back for the bonfire tonight." He opened the door to leave.

"Oh yeah, Mom," River exclaimed as she bounced into the room. "Jazz, Charlie and Josh are coming over for a bonfire tonight."

Patti smiled at her daughter. "Okay, that's cool. Just let Randy know, and he can get some firewood for you. See you tonight, Josh."

River smiled back at Josh as he left. Her smile vanished when Randy stormed into the kitchen and slammed the door behind him. River's mom took a deep breath, but only River heard her.

Here we go, River thought.

"What the hell, River," Randy started in, "Why are the wet saddle blankets on the front porch still? I thought I told you to hang them up right away?"

"Yeah . . . I was going to . . ." River grumbled. "But then Mom called us in for dinner." She started to set the table.

Trying to explain just made Randy more aggressive. "Why do you always have a snarky attitude?"

Randy picked up a plate and smashed it against the brick chimney beside the dinner table. He picked up another and smashed it too. Blood dripped from his hand and splattered onto the plate River was still holding.

River slouched into a chair. She sat in silence until Randy had finished his tantrum. How he hated her mom's choice of music, teenagers with attitudes and eating the same damn dinner every night. After he stomped to the basement, she heard the bottles clinking as he rummaged through them. He stomped up the stairs and out the door. She listened to the sound of the truck speeding away down the driveway.

She saw tears staining her mom's cheeks. Her mom bent to pick up some of the larger pieces that remained of the plates that had belonged to her grandmother. She placed them carefully in the garbage can. River opened the closet door, grabbed the vacuum and plugged it in. She stopped and shrugged. Tears welled in the corners of her eyes. She hugged her mom.

"Mom. Are you okay?" River whispered.

Her mom said nothing. She wept. She wiped her tears with her sleeve like a child.

"Mom? Why does he do this all the time? Aren't you sick of this?" River pleaded. "Seriously, we're running out of Nana's dishes for him to smash," she said with a nervous laugh.

Her mom looked surprised at her comment, but she chuckled anyway. "I have no idea how you have a sense of humour through all of this. I can't believe I make you live through this. I am so sorry. It really has to stop." She took a deep breath. "I have something to tell you." She bit her bottom lip.

"Okay . . ." They had been through this all before, but this part was new.

"River, I can't do this anymore. I want to do what's best for you. I want you to be happy and safe. You're becoming a woman. And I don't want you thinking that this kind of relationship is okay. It's not healthy at all. Just because he doesn't hit me, it still doesn't make it okay."

They were both quiet for a minute. To River, it felt like ten.

"Oh hell," her mom muttered. "River, I've been seeing someone else!"

River was sure she had heard her mom wrong. Her mind raced. *She's . . . been . . . seeing . . . someone . . . else . . .*

River saw her mom's lips moving, but to River her voice sounded muffled. It was as if she was in the other room. "He's a native guy from the rez. His name is Thomas. He said we could live there with him. I thought it might be a good idea, since you know, you're struggling a bit with who you are . . . and . . ."

"Wait, what?" River scrunched her eyebrows. For some reason she found herself laughing.

She listened to her mom ramble. "He has a ponytail. And he has four kids, who are all older than you, and only two live with him. Two boys and two girls. And his home is a beautiful spot among the trees. You'll only be half an hour away from Trent. So you won't have to live in residence. We won't be able to afford residence now, anyway."

River sat up in the chair with a blank stare. The lump in her throat felt like a tennis ball. This was all going too fast.

"Mom," she said, cutting off her mom's description of the reserve where Thomas lived. "I think I need to be alone for a few minutes."

She crept up the stairs and flopped onto the bed. She landed on her stomach with her face in the pillow. She didn't know what to feel — anger, sadness, relief? She knew what the words meant. But she couldn't figure out what it meant for her mom, for her. For their life. It sounded to River like her mom had already made up her mind and had a master plan all figured out. The one thing she forgot to do was talk to River about it.

CHAPTER 4

I Fight Myself

Half an hour later, River walked steadily downstairs. Her mom was standing at the kitchen sink. She gazed out the window at the sunset hovering above the corn fields.

"Thanks, Mom, for giving me some time," River whispered. She hugged her mom around the waist from behind. Her cheek was flat against her mom's back. "It's just all so sudden. Like, I hoped in my heart this was coming, but the surprise shocked me. You could have told me we were moving, you know. And then told me about your new boyfriend a few days later. You could have like, taken me out for pizza before you tried to sweet talk me into moving away from my favourite guy Randy."

"River!" her mom scolded as she laughed through her tears.

"Seriously, Mom. I know this must be really hard for you." She squeezed her mom tighter. Her mom squeezed back. Then she turned and held River's cheeks in the palms of her hands.

"Let's go get some pizza." Her mom smiled. She reached for her purse and her keys, and they made their way to the car.

* * *

"I'll have a diet coke and a personal pan pizza — Hawaiian, please," River said. She didn't even bother looking at the menu.

"I'll have the same, but an iced tea rather than a diet coke," said her mom. She placed the menus at the side of table, gesturing for the waitress to take them with her.

"Perfect," squeaked the young woman. "I'll be right back with your drinks." River could see that she was trying too hard for a tip.

River placed both of her palms down in front of her on the table of their booth. She leaned forward.

"Legit, Mom?" she said in a low voice. "You really want to pack up, leave Randy and go live on the rez with Thomas? Like, when did this even happen? How did this happen? Where did you meet him?" She took her glass from the hands of the waitress. She puckered fish lips around the straw and blew a few bubbles, trying to make her mother laugh.

"River, stop." Her mom fought down a smile. "Thomas really is a wonderful soul, Riv. I think you're really going to like him. I met him at a powwow last summer. He is an artist and I fell in love with his art. He is Cree, and he reminds me of your dad a bit. He's soft and kind, and he's a good listener. Well, your dad was soft and kind, but he was a terrible listener. I don't know, I guess I'm a sucker for that Cree humour and long braids. Anyway, Thomas is really looking forward to meeting you. He knows some of the struggles you are going through. He said it must be tough being the only native girl in a small town. He gets it."

"People don't say native anymore Mom. It's 'Indigenous' now."

"You know what I mean, Riv," she replied.

The waitress came back with their pizza. "Thank you," River's mom said quietly. As the waitress walked swiftly away from the table, River's mom paused for a response.

River toyed with the straw in her glass. She finally broke her silence. "Mom, what really happened between you and Dad? Hell, what really happened between you and Randy?"

"I left your dad because he just wasn't there. It's not just that he travelled all the time, doing who knows what. I tried to give him his freedom. But even when he was home, he wasn't really there, you know? We never talked. He never told me things to help me understand him. After you were born, I asked him about his family, about his past. I wanted anything he could tell me that would let us help you grow up in both our cultures. Whenever I tried to talk about anything he would be quiet or leave the room. I could never really read him."

"I know the type," River mumbled. She thought about how good her mom had been at keeping her own secrets.

"It was like I was drowning in silence. I felt alone all the time. It felt like we were roommates, not husband and wife. And with him away from home so much, it didn't even hit me until a couple of months after I left him that we were actually separated. I just finally made the decision that I wanted to be happy. Because if I wasn't happy, I wasn't going to raise a happy child."

River didn't know how she felt about being one of the reasons her parents had split up.

"About six months after I realized your dad and I were done, I met Randy at your uncle's birthday party. I was having a really hard time with you, doing it all on my own. Randy was stable, had a job and made me laugh. We had a lot of fun together. At first the drinking was just on the weekends. It wasn't a problem for years. When it got bad enough, I thought I could change him. I started nagging him to quit, and things just got worse from there. By that time, I could see how living on the farm was good for you. You loved the animals and made friends. I didn't want to leave this all behind. I didn't want you to have to change schools, and it just never felt like the right time to leave."

So why now? thought River. She felt even worse that she was one of the reasons her mom stayed with Randy.

"I felt like I lost myself again. I didn't even know who I was anymore. It's been over with Randy for a long time, but it took even longer this time to leave. Then I met Thomas last year. I started feeling like myself again. I know a man shouldn't determine how I feel. But I just felt so much like my old self when I was around him. I fell in love with that feeling, and wanted to be around him more and more. And I was thankful to him that I could love myself again. But then things just kind of changed. I never really meant for it to go like that. It just did."

River's mom took a sip of her iced tea. River could tell she had surprised herself by telling the whole story at once.

"Mom, I can't believe you haven't told me any of this," said River. "I've been old enough to hear it for a while now. Just yesterday at the beach, me and Charlie and Jazz and Josh were talking about being caught between parents in a divorce. The worst thing is to not know what's going on."

Suddenly, River felt guilty. It wasn't like she had shared things with her mom a lot in the last while. She had been freaking out a little over what was going to happen when she went to her dad's. And about what it would be like going to school in the fall. But she never said anything to her mom.

"Okay, River," said her mom. "What do you want to talk about?"

Why not? River thought. "Did I ever tell you how I felt when I was being bullied about being 'native' when I was little?" She used her fingers to make quotation marks in the air.

"You were bullied about being *native*? When? By *who*?" her mom demanded.

"Remember when I came home asking questions about Eskimos and drunk people and Indians on welfare?" River's eyes were wide.

"Yes, I remember that. I knew you had heard it from somewhere. But you said friends were saying that. And you never told me about being bullied. And is it really even called bullying, or should we call it what it was? RACISM." River's mom finally turned to her pizza.

"Well, whatever we decide to call it, it happened all the time." River bit into her own pizza, surprised that she was hungry enough to eat it.

"The only thing I remember you telling me about was in grade three. You know, when Mrs. Green was poking you and Sarah on the head."

"Oh my god, yes! She wouldn't do it to anyone else in the class. If Sarah and I were talking or something, she would make a peace sign." River held up two fingers. "And then she would use her fingers to poke us in the top of the head. She slapped me on the legs one day too. It was in gym class. I was sitting on the stage, swinging my legs, and she came along and slapped me. Maybe I was talking or something, or just swinging my legs. But it was only ever me and Sarah she treated like that. The ONLY two Indigenous kids in the class, and in the *whole* school."

"Yes, and I reported her to the school. And to the Human Rights Commission."

"Well, good. She was so cranky. Who could believe a teacher would still be that racist. And with kids? It messed me up for a while. I wanted to be white, Mom. Or at least, not brown. That's why I wanted to cut my hair really short too." River's eyes dimmed with sadness.

"Oh, honey, I had no idea." River could see her mom's eyes held a different kind of sadness. "I had no idea it affected you this much. Is there anything I can do to help?"

"Not really. It's just something I have to work through I guess. I still feel like something is always missing. Like, I'm happy, but never a hundred per cent happy. I don't think I'm depressed. It's different. It's like I'm waiting for something exciting to happen, but it never comes. Or sometimes I feel like I'm in this constant state of resistance, but I don't know what I'm resisting. I just know my body feels tense when I think about it too much."

Her mom nodded. "I know the feeling. It sounds like you are ready to do a little soul searching of your own. It's completely normal for you to feel like that, especially at your age. But as you can tell from what I've been telling you, people feel it at all different ages. And it's different for everyone. When you're older, some call it a mid-life crisis. You need to find the thing or feeling that makes you truly happy and content. And it's not something anyone but you can figure out."

"Hmm. Okay, so while I'm out soul searching, what are you going to do? What are we even going to say to Randy? He's going to lose his mind when he finds out we're leaving."

"We're not saying anything to Randy. I've got a plan in place, a way for both of us to leave safely. We're doing a midnight move. I have a trailer lined up and your uncles will come and help. We'll move everything we want to take during the night while Randy is at work. That way we avoid any more drama. I know it seems really crazy right now. But once we are all settled in, I promise it will be different. Our lives might feel normal again. No more walking on egg shells, wondering when the next set of dishes will smash against the wall."

"Okay, Mom," River said, but her voice was filled with doubt. "But I still think it's happening way too fast. What about my stuff? How will I pack up my stuff without Randy noticing?" River's chest was feeling a little tight.

"Well, this week, make sure you put the special things you want to take with you in a box in your closet. It won't be too obvious because you're packing to go away for the summer to your dad's, and to go to Trent in the fall. I've been telling Randy I'm purging a bunch of stuff and donating it to the thrift store. Pack the rest of the important things in the extra suitcase that's in your closet and put it under your bed. Then all the bedding and furniture will be moved the day of."

"Geez, it all sounds so cold, Mom."

"It has to be this way when you live with an abusive and alcoholic partner. You never know when they are going to blow. I do know for sure that if Randy knew we were leaving he would lose his mind. So we take the safest option. It's called a safety plan."

"Geez, Mom, I'm really sorry you have to go through this."

"I know, River. And I'm sorry you do too." She waved down the waitress and placed her bank card on the scuffed black tray to pay the bill.

"So when is this midnight move supposed to happen?" River blinked, trying to stop tears from leaving her eyes.

"The Saturday after you go to your dad's in Winnipeg. I don't want you to be there."

River's stomach sank. "I kind of wish I wasn't going back home now," she said.

River's mom put her arm around her as they walked to the car. "We are going to get through this, River," she said. "What doesn't kill you makes you stronger."

River wished she could believe that.

June 22

Sooo. Where do I even start? This situation with Randy and my mom is something. Those two are so messed up it's crazy. I'm still in shock that my mom is just packing up the house and moving to the reserve. I can't even imagine it. I wonder what they even do there. I wonder what people are like? I wonder if I will live there or will I end up going to residence? All of a sudden no money?! Now what?

I'm crying. Again. I don't think I've cried this much since grade five.

I just want to get away. What if I visit my dad in Winnipeg and just stay there? What if I just move out there with him for a while? It could be a new beginning away from it all. I have no idea what tomorrow will bring. Maybe when I wake up, it will all have been just a bad dream.

Wishful thinking, much?

Maybe, if this is really happening, I should start thinking about how I am going to get to class in the fall. If I can't stay in residence, and I don't have a car, what am I going to do?

I wonder if I should defer my school acceptance for a year. If I did that, then staying at my dad's house for a year might actually work.

GIIKAANDOOG

CHAPTER 5

We Quarrel with Each Other

The laundry basket bounced on the bed. River folded her lavender-scented clothes and sorted them into piles according to her list. She looked around the room and had no idea where to begin with everything else. She thought the easiest way to start might be with things she knew she was getting rid of. She needed a clear bag to get rid of old papers, and another for old makeup containers. She had to tackle the stuff in a 'to be sorted' pile in the corner of her closet. She had several plastic water bottles in her room that were still half full. As she placed the bottles in a blue bag, she thought about how bad they were for the environment. She knew she had to stop using them. She just had a hard time following through on stuff like that.

She was thankful she had watched *Hoarders* on TV. She didn't feel so bad. When she got overwhelmed with the task, she reminded herself that, since there weren't dead animals in her room, she was ahead of the game.

She walked around the room again, and placed all the things she was definitely keeping in a box. She piled up the clothes she would be taking to Winnipeg, and started a bag of clothes that were too small or out of style. She thought her little cousins might like them. That made her smile a few times. Her little cousins, who looked up to her, loved getting hand-me-down clothes from her. River wondered if she should be bringing her farm-ish clothes to Thomas's rez. They might not think that her plaid shirt and ripped skinny jeans were cool. Then she started to wonder if she might not be accepted on the rez. What if she didn't make any friends at school either? She thought of sitting alone all weekend while everyone in residence was having fun without her. While Josh was having fun without her. She rubbed her eyes, then grabbed the pillow beside her to cover her face. She screamed into it and then whipped it across the room. It hit the wall with a quiet thud. She stood up and continued packing.

River started going through the art supplies she had collected over the years. Her art table was full of half-finished pieces, mostly of dark drawings. Trees and young women falling from trees — a recurring theme. She had a few pieces of unfinished beadwork. A pair of half-finished moccasins she had started in grade eight. Two beaded hair clips that she had started and didn't like so never finished. A pair of beaded blingy earrings like the girls wore at powwows that needed to be fixed around the edge. She had no idea what to do with it all. It felt weird and disrespectful to throw it out. Finally, she stuffed it all into a box and wrote BEADS on the outside. Like everything else, she would deal with it later.

She finished tidying her room and took a photo she found of her mom downstairs to show her. Her mom was sitting on the couch in the living room, folding dish towels.

"Mom, where was this picture taken?" River passed it to her mom and sat beside her on the couch.

Her mom reached for the photo and wrinkled her brow. "Hmm. Geez, I think this is me and your uncle. I think we were about seventeen here? Grandma had a couple of horses, and we would go riding on the weekends. Ha! Kind of like you and Josh."

"Except me and Josh are way cooler, and not, like, related."

"Of course you are way cooler, my darling," her mom responded kindly. "Did you get a chance to tell Josh about everything going on?"

"Mom, I can't even. I just finished packing my room. I don't want to talk about it."

"River, you have been saying that a lot lately. I don't want you shutting me out."

River didn't answer.

"You know, Riv, I know this is a lot for you to handle. But getting angry and holding it in isn't going to help. You need to talk about it."

"Where's Randy?" River asked.

"He went to get hay and straw. He'll be back in about an hour."

River's emotions were all over the place. Anger with her mom. Sadness for her mom. Anger at Randy, and then sadness for him too. Anxiety that she didn't know what her future would hold.

"I am upstairs packing my room in secret so your psychotic husband doesn't find out. I'm putting memories of my childhood into a *box*, and I have no idea where this box is going. It's not like I got a say in where we were moving to. It's not like I got to pick out the bedroom I'll be sleeping in once we move. Oh, wait a minute. Do I even *have* a bedroom?"

River's mom's arms were crossed against her chest. But she let River go on.

"I have to leave my animals, my horse. I have to leave my home. What do I have to look forward to? Watching you be in love with your new boyfriend?" Tears ran down River's cheeks.

Finally, River's mom spoke. "You know, honey, I thought I was doing the right thing. That keeping the decisions away from you would help keep some of the stress from you too. I didn't realize that there were so many unknowns for you. I have just been trying to focus on keeping you safe and happy. All I could think about was getting you away from here and to somewhere peaceful. Maybe with new friends and people you can connect to culturally. I don't know, Riv . . . I'm really sorry. I'm trying my best here." She sighed and wiped her tears. "We have to stick together during this rough patch."

"I can't deal, Mom. There is so much stuff I am going through right now. Stuff with Josh, and school. And figuring out how a half breed is supposed to fit in. And now this. This has just pushed me over the edge. Like, *Bon-voyage, River. Jump off this cliff into the abyss, River. See you on the other side, River!*"

Her mom looked more confused than ever. "Whoa, River, what do you mean, half breed? Where did *that* come from?"

"Mom, I'm a half breed. Get over it."

"I never thought you would use such an ugly term for yourself. Is that why you are so *angry* lately?"

"You just asked me to not hold in my feelings. And then I tell you my feelings. And then you get upset that one of the feelings is anger?"

Her mom exploded. "You know, River, when I was your age, I never got a say either. Sometimes you just don't get a god damn say, no matter how old you are. And you get over it!"

River stormed upstairs. She tossed some clothes into her backpack, and ran back down the stairs. Glaring at her mom, who had returned to folding towels, River left and slammed the door behind her.

AAKDEHEWIN

CHAPTER 6

Courage

The pebbles beneath River's feet seemed to crunch louder than ever before. She had thought about what she could do to take control of her life. She had forced herself to calm down before she came to say goodbye to the animals.

She gently set her backpack down at the barn door. She sang, "Hey, little bunnies, where aarre youuu?" Three grey bunnies, each not much bigger than a deck of cards, hopped out from beneath their mother. She cuddled them into one ball of bunny fur in her arms. They were very shy, but River had fed them from her hands since the day she was allowed to touch them.

"Okay, little guys, you have to be brave now. I won't be seeing you anymore. You will have to take care of each other." Her voice got higher. "Don't let anyone get cold. Be kind to your siblings. Always eat your vegetables so you can grow up to be big and strong, okay?" She set them down one by one. They hopped around, leaving little black pellets in their tracks.

River walked over to the trough. "See ya later, Miss Piggy." She scratched the sow on her head. "You're the best. You're the smartest pig I know. One day you will probably be very tasty." She was trying to use humour to alleviate the pain in her throat, the pain in her heart. But she knew it was just a mask, and maybe the animals did too.

River took a deep breath and walked around to the side of the barn. Her horse, Juniper, was standing in the corral, a little sweaty from dancing around with General and Janey. Juniper heard the click from the side of River's cheek, the universal call for horses. Juniper's head stood erect, and she neighed the loudest neigh River had ever heard. The only other time Juniper had neighed so loud was when a coyote was jumping the fence.

Tears welled up in River's eyes. *It's like she knows*, River thought as she sobbed.

River put her arms around her mare's neck and squeezed as tight as she could. She used only her fingertips to touch the length of Juniper's nose. She scratched her horse's chin a little and tried to avoid the constant licks from her tongue. River grabbed the cell phone from her back pocket and took a selfie with Juniper. She cried as she looked at the photo. She buried her face in Juniper's neck again, and sobbed. "I don't know what I'm going to do without you guys. My whole world is turning upside down. I'm leaving you behind. And the saddest part is that you will think it's because I don't love you. I want you to know that this is not my choice, Juniper. I would never leave you behind by choice. I love you."

River felt a little dizzy, so she sat down under a tree outside the barn to call an Uber.

"Hi. I'm looking for a pick up. I live on a farm, so I can ping you my location. Can you pick me up at the end of my road? . . . Okay, hang on . . . okay, did you get it . . . Right, half an hour."

River had made up her mind. She would visit her friend Shaylee in Calgary. If Shaylee couldn't put her up, she could crash at her uncle Don's place. She picked up her backpack and walked toward the main highway. All the way, she resisted the urge to look behind her.

* * *

River's mind raced. She ignored her mom's panicked question. She walked to the ticket booth and smiled sheepishly at the woman behind the bullet-proof glass. The woman looked as if she was having a rough day. She wore blue latex gloves, and had a coffee stain on her uniform. She looked at River impatiently.

"Yeah, can, uh, can I have a one-way ticket to Calgary please?" River asked. "The night bus."

The woman's fingers flew so fast over the keyboard, it looked fake, like she wasn't typing at all. *Maybe it's the gloves*, River thought. The unhappy woman handed her a bus ticket.

"Thank you." River smiled nervously as she struggled to put her bank card back in her wallet.

"What's in Calgary, dear?" the woman asked.

River looked stunned. "Oh, uh, just visiting family for the summer."

"Ah, yes, lots of kids travelling to visit family this time of year."

"Yeah," River said.

The woman smiled. "Your bus leaves in an hour."

River smiled back. "Thank you." She walked over to the big window and people-watched for a few minutes. She bought a few snacks and went to the washroom. She opened her journal as she waited for her bus.

June 23, Bus Station

The bus ticket to Calgary was only $300. I have more than enough money to last me all summer. And there is no way I'm responding to Mom right now. I'm so angry that she's making all of these big changes without even involving me. I have no control over anything. I don't even know this new boyfriend that I'm supposed to just go live with.

I feel like I'm going to have a meltdown like a toddler right now. I just want to throw myself on the floor and kick and scream and cry. And I want to wait there until someone comes along and swoops me up in their arms, and hugs me. I'll wrap my legs around their waist, and lay my head on their shoulder as I sniffle. I imagine that's what it feels like to have a full-time dad. I've never felt that. Someone scooping me up and hugging me and telling me it's all going to be okay. That they will never leave my side. That they will love me no matter what I do or say, even if it's not that nice. Never. Not once. And that's what dads are supposed to do. Well, I think anyway.

GAWIIN NGII-NSASTAZGOZIZII

CHAPTER 7

I am Misunderstood

Though relieved to have two seats to herself, River felt tingles of loneliness in her chest. The hum of the air conditioner beneath the seat in front of her made it difficult to fall asleep. The hum of snoring at the back of the bus made it even more difficult to *stay* asleep. It had only been eight hours, and they weren't even to Sault Ste. Marie yet.

River saw a man walking to the restroom at the back of the bus. After tossing and turning in her seat, she got up to stretch her legs. She glanced at her phone. Four in the morning. She wondered if taking the red eye was really the best idea, even though it was the cheapest. She walked to the back of the bus and stood patiently waiting for the man to exit. He had been in there for quite a while, and she thought about sitting back down. When the door opened, the person outlined by the door caught her gaze. But in the restroom, the man had transformed into a woman. They were no longer wearing track pants and a hoodie, but had on black shiny tights, a purple tunic and a scarf adorned with embroidered flowers. *The makeup is AH-MAZING*, River thought. She smiled as they walked past her to sit down.

River locked the door and leaned against the tiny stainless-steel sink. It was full of long brown hair. She stared into the mirror and wiped the sleep from the corner of her eyes. She grabbed her toothbrush from her travel bag and dabbed a little paste on top, balancing with her legs spread apart as the bus turned a wide corner. She peered into the sink as she brushed and thought about how many germs were around her at that very moment. She felt gross. She spat out her toothpaste and washed her hands. She had trouble unlocking the restroom door from the inside, so she fiddled and twisted until the door finally blew open. She slouched back into her seat while covering herself in hand sanitizer.

She turned off the airplane mode on her cell phone. A string of messages rang through. She glanced at them and rolled her eyes, as she skimmed through them.

Mom: River where are you?

Josh: Riv, your mom just called me. Please call us, we're worried about you! Where are you? Baby, please call me.

Jasmine: River, what the hoo-ha, where are you!?

Charlotte: RIVER. CALL ME.

Dad: Hey hunny, it's Dad. Please call me when you get this message.

Nokomis: Hey, my girl, it's Nokomis. I'm worried sick. Please call me just to tell me you are okay.

River thought about how her nokomis, her dad's mother, Grace, used to sing to her in her language when she was small. She thought about the summer star blanket quilts she used to curl up in while her nokomis read stories to her and told her children's tales from long ago. She always knew that her nokomis wanted to pass down as many stories as she could, keeping the tradition of oral storytelling alive. Her nokomis told River that one day, when she was a grandmother herself, she would have lots of stories to tell her grandbabies. She thought about how her nokomis was probably still awake, worrying about her. River couldn't bear the thought of keeping her up and out of sorts.

River hugged her travel pillow and responded to her nokomis. Her thumbs on her phone were swift as she typed.

River: Good morning, Nokomis. I'm okay. I'm on a Greyhound, taking the bus to Calgary. Please don't tell anyone. Or at least, can you wait till I get there? I'm going to stay with Uncle Don and the kids. I love you.

River: Hello, my girl. What can I say that will help you? Will you please call me? I'm so worried about you.

River: Okay, I'll call you at our next stop so I don't wake everyone.

River: Oh thank you, my girl. I will have to tell your dad you are okay though.

River: Okay, Noki. <3

* * *

Nokomis picked up the phone on the first ring. The birds had started praying already. Dawn wouldn't come for another hour.

"Hi, River. How are you doing, sweetheart? You must be so tired!"

"Yeah, I'm okay, Noki, I just really need some sleep."

"Whereabouts are you, dear?"

"Um . . . I can't remember where the bus driver said we were . . ."

"Oh, River, you have everyone worried sick. They almost called the police, you know, to report you missing."

"Oh, really? I didn't think anyone would notice I was gone." Her voice was flat.

"My girl, you know that's not true." River could hear the worry and fatigue in her grandmother's voice.

"Noki, I'm so sorry to have worried you. Mom and I had a big fight. She's moving out of Randy's house, which is good I guess, but she's moving us in with another man I haven't met. All my stuff is in boxes, and I had to leave my animals. I feel like I'm falling apart, Noki. I don't know what to do. I just wanted to get on a bus and get away from it all."

Her nokomis's voice was soft. It was always gentle and kind. It didn't matter what time of day or night. "Oh, my girl, I'm so sorry you are going through all of this. You know, it might be a good idea for you to get off the bus in Winnipeg. Just come and stay with us. It's what we had planned for later anyway. We'd be happy to have you a bit early! It sounds like you really need someone to talk to."

"Yeah, I guess. I don't know. I don't want to bother you and Dad with this stuff. I thought it might be weird for you guys."

"We're all adults, my girl. We can handle it."

"You're right, Noki" River said after a long pause. "Okay. I'll get off the bus in Winnipeg. I don't know how long it will take us to get there though."

"It's okay, dear. I'll have your dad look it up on the inter-web, and he can figure it out. We will be at the bus station when you arrive."

"All right, Noki. Thank you."

"Oh my sweet girl, giizagun."

"I love you too, Noki."

June 24, I Think

I love how my nokomis calls me "my girl." Everyone in Dad's family calls me that. They call all the young girls that, come to think of it. I never thought about it, but it must be a cultural thing.

I'm not sure how much journaling I can do on this bus. I thought I would have lots more time to figure things out. I guess I'm getting off in Winnipeg. I can't bear the thought of upsetting Nokomis any more.

I remember when I was about seven and Mom was marrying Randy. I couldn't understand why Mom and Dad couldn't just get married to each other again. Nokomis spent so much time telling me about love, and how love is meant to be kind, and not full of anger and mistrust.

Part of my problem is that I'm not sure how I feel about anything anymore. Most of the time, I'm happy. But something is definitely missing. I feel like I'm searching for something. But I don't even know what it is I'm looking for. I guess I'm hoping I can just go somewhere and find the answer. Emerge a whole new something, like the person I saw just now on the bus. Maybe spending time with Nokomis and learning more about my Native side will help me with that.

I don't know. I'm too tired to think this one through. The snoring behind me isn't helping either.

GWAAJDAABII

CHAPTER 8

Drag Something Out of the Water

River's father, Eric, stood patiently in the arrival section of the bus terminal. River walked through the doors and dropped her bag to the floor. She wrapped her arms around his neck. Despite the large dark circles under her eyes, she smiled from ear to ear as her dad squeezed.

"Ohh it's so good to see you, my girl." Eric's voice was muffled by her hair.

"Haww good to see you too, Dad," she whispered as she squeezed a little tighter.

"C'mon, let's get your bags. Your nokomis is waiting for you in the car."

"Oh good, I can't wait to see her!"

"Yeah, she's excited to see you too."

The dirty terminal floor was marked with arrows pointing to the exit. River placed her arm through her dad's and they made their way to the parking lot.

"Nokomis! It's so good to see you!" River slid into the back behind the passenger's seat where Grace, her nokomis, was sitting and squeezed her shoulders.

Grace laid her wrinkled hand atop River's and kissed it. "You too, my girl. How are you?" she asked in a frail, tired voice.

"Oh, it was pretty uneventful. A bit noisy from all the snoring. But I was finally able to sleep for a couple of hours after I talked to you."

"When we get back to the rez, you can have a nice long bath and a good night's sleep in a comfy bed. Twenty-six hours on a bus is a long time! Are you hungry? Eric, let's go through a drive thru for burgers or something. Your girls need to be fed."

"Sure, Mom," replied Eric. "I know the perfect place. River, it's a burger joint and it's over by the Long Plains Urban Reserve. It's a little out of the way but it's worth it. They serve bannock with their burgers."

"What's an urban reserve, Dad?" River asked around a huge yawn.

"Oh, right, well, in short, it's land in the city that becomes part of the reserve."

"I must be way too tired for a history lesson, Dad. That just went in one ear and right out the other. Sorry." She yawned again.

"Yeah, no worries dear, we have all summer for me to tell you about treaties, and the treaty system in Canada."

"Sounds exciting," River said with a smile. At the same time, she shook her head no, making her nokomis giggle.

They drove in silence for a few minutes.

"Okay, young ladies, here's the burger place I was talking about. I'll go order and I'll be right back." Eric pulled into the parking lot and turned the car off, leaving the windows rolled down.

River leaned into the seat in front of her. "Noki, on the bus I realized that I need your help with something. I'm trying to figure some things out, and it might help if I knew more. You know, about our people and our culture. How do I learn about all this stuff Dad knows? There's no one to talk to about any of this where I live." She thought about how that all might change when she moved to the reserve. Then she pushed that thought out of her mind when her emotions surged up.

"Well, River my girl, do you have a native centre near your house? Maybe you could visit some Elders there. You could do that here too. You'll meet some of your family at the powwow. Or there's a youth centre in the city you could visit. They do all sorts of cultural things, language classes, beading classes, teachings with Elders. Heck, even bingo too."

They laughed together. River had almost forgotten how good it felt.

"And then there's me," her nokomis went on. "I could share a few stories or two. Lord knows I have stories. And juicy ones."

"Noki, you're the best. I'd love to hear your stories. All of them. And especially the juicy ones," River giggled.

"All right. We can start tomorrow night, after you are all caught up on your rest. Your noki loves drinking tea and telling stories. You know storytelling has always been the way we pass on knowledge to the younger generation. I bet your dad has some good stories too. He probably has some not so good stories to tell, unfortunately. But I'll let him tell you the sad ones. Your noki doesn't want to tell sad stories anymore. I have told way too many in my lifetime. Seen too much."

"I get it, Noki. It's okay, you don't have to tell me those ones."

Eric hopped back into the car and handed out the food. "Dig in gals," Eric instructed, as he turned the keys and put the car into drive. He adjusted his rear-view mirror to smile at his daughter.

They passed the Red River and the volunteers in boats. They were using what looked to be large chains and farm equipment.

"What are they doing, Dad?" River asked.

"Uhh . . . well. Have you heard in the media about the young woman who went missing in Winnipeg last week?"

"No." River looked concerned. "What happened to her? What does that have to do with the river?"

"There's a movement here in Winnipeg called Drag the Red. It was actually started by an old friend of mine, whose sister went missing a long time ago. She wanted to find answers. They search the Red River for clues, since the bodies of so many of our sisters have been disposed of there."

"Oh my god. I just lost my appetite." River shoved the crumpled bag of food beside her.

"I'm sorry, babe. We can talk about it later."

"Okay," she replied, feeling a bit numb.

The hour drive back to the rez didn't seem too long. The landscape was the same almost the entire drive down Highway 75. Flat, with endless plains and the odd barn silo. It looked like the farmlands she was used to, except there were more trees in Ontario.

River opened her journal and placed her pencil on the clean page. She wrote quickly before the sun started setting.

June 25, In The Car

All right, so this is not how I thought my first meeting up with my dad and Noki would go. It's like I just woke up from a bad dream into another one. I've heard about missing and murdered Indigenous girls and women. But when you actually drive past something like people dragging the Red River, the hairs on your arms stand up. It's chilling to imagine that a body could pop up at any moment while you're out in those boats with those chains. I would be sick to my stomach. I feel sick just thinking about it.

I wonder who she was. The young girl who went missing. She probably had a family. A mom. A dad. Someone must have loved her. She must have had hopes and dreams like me. Oh my god, it could totally be me out there. What if I went missing? No wonder Dad and Noki were so worried about me.

Sheesh. I didn't realize until right now how my mom is probably feeling. And Josh. And my friends. Randy probably didn't even notice I was gone.

NIIBIISHAABOOKE MIINWAA
SASGOKWAADENS NGA-ZHITOON

CHAPTER 9

I'll Make Tea and Bannock

River noticed the changes when they passed the 'welcome to the reserve' sign. There were houses that looked like shacks right beside the landscaped yards of brand new houses. Dogs ran with no collars and junk was strewn on lawns. There were more than a few old cars jacked up in driveways with tires missing. She could tell which houses had children, because toys and bikes and clothes were scattered about. Some of the gravel driveways were filled with puddles and large potholes.

Her nokomis's yard was neatly kept. Her home was older, but she kept the white vinyl siding clean and bright. River remembered the flowers blooming in a clay pot on the cement stairs. Lace curtains were pulled in every window.

River shuffled her bags inside and felt the stale air meet her lungs. She was used to no air conditioning, but the breeze on the farm always made up for it. The heat was different in the plains. It was dry and stuffy.

She hefted her suitcase up onto the bed of the guest room. There was an old brown wooden dresser and a night stand with a fragile lamp. Under the lamp was an ivory doily that her nokomis had probably crocheted herself. River looked for an outlet to charge her phone.

She sat on the edge of the bed beside a doll with a large knitted skirt that was half the size of the bed. She poked it and its eyes wiggled, then the left eye stuck shut. "*Oh so creepy,*" River whispered to herself. She laid the doll face down in the corner of the room. She had to wrestle with it a bit. Its legs kept sticking out and she got tangled in the skirt. River gave the doll a little kick with her toes just to make sure it wasn't really alive. She changed into a clean pair of pyjamas, staring at the doll the whole time, hoping it wouldn't peek out and look at her. Finally, River laughed at herself and stepped out of the bedroom. She shut the bedroom door and made her way down the narrow stairs covered in baby blue shag carpet.

"The tea is on." Her nokomis was nestled in her rocking chair. "We were going to tell stories this evening, Eric. But maybe River should get some rest instead."

"Oh, Noki, I'm okay," said River. "I got a second wind. Really, I'm wide awake right now. Kind of excited to see you. And I had a little cat nap in the car too."

"Okay. Well, come sit down and join us, my dear."

River sat on the couch next to her nokomis's chair. She brought her knees to her chest, looking at the nail polish on her toes that needed to be redone.

"Absolutely," Eric agreed.

"Hey, Dad," said River. "Noki said you can tell the sad stories and she'll tell the juicy stories."

Eric raised his eyebrows at his mother. "She did, did she? Well I'll let her start. Then we can see if there's time before bed for some melancholy. I'll get us some tea. I think there's some bannock left over from earlier."

"Okay, my girl, where shall I start?" her nokomis asked.

"Tell me about how you met Mishomis. What was it like dating back then?"

"Ahhh, very good place to start, my girl." River settled in as her nokomis began in her soft voice. "Well, dating rules back then on the rez were probably not the same as they were off the rez. We couldn't even leave the reserve without a pass, so we always had to sneak around. The teenagers would hang out behind the old church when we came home from school at Christmas time. It was sheltered from the wind there. Adults never went near the graveyard after dark, so it was the perfect spot. My cousin Hazel had an old radio, and we used to listen to music when we could find batteries. One night, some teenage boys snuck out from the next reserve over through the back trails, and met up with us. It was so exciting to meet other young people from a different community. When we were small we thought we were the only Natives on the planet!"

River smiled as she grabbed her cup. She slurped her iced tea loudly.

Her nokomis laughed and went on. "Anyway, that was the night I met your grandfather. He was two years older than me. And, boy, was he handsome. We didn't keep long hair then, since the rule was no long hair at school. Clan systems or any kind of traditions were supposed to be illegal. But we just kept them secret. That's how everyone knew who they were related to. You had to know your clan so you didn't marry your cousin!" She laughed really hard at this.

"So what clan are we, Noki?"

"We are deer clan. Waawaashkeshig. We also don't eat our own clan. You never eat deer meat if you are from the deer clan."

River nodded. *Note to self. No venison*, she thought. "What clan was Mishomis?" she asked.

Eric yelled from the other room, "SKUNK CLAN. HE STUNK ALL THE TIME."

49

River laughed. Her nokomis nodded in agreement, her eyes wide with laughter. "He did stink. But I'm certain he was loon clan. He was a water baby, just like you. He liked to be alone a lot on the river. Always wanting to be near the water. I think that's why your dad wanted to call you River, because of your grandfather."

Eric stuck his head around the corner and smiled at his daughter, nodding to confirm his mother's words.

"That's sweet. I didn't know I was named after him, or his personality I guess." River smiled back.

"His spirit," her nokomis said, with gentle eyes. "You were definitely named after his spirit. Anyways, back to my love story . . . That night it started to storm out of nowhere. We had been home from school just for a few days, and so everyone was still wearing their best clothes. We weren't dressed very warm, but nobody wanted to go home. Well, it got so bad that we could barely see in front of us. We didn't want to get caught sneaking out, so we hid the four young men in the barn with the chickens that night. I remember it like it was yesterday. Your grandfather picked up a little white feather and threw it to me. It seemed to float through the air, much further than it should have. It landed right behind my ear." She smiled as she continued.

"We snuck those boys blankets and warm tea and bannock. In the morning we went to check on them. But they were already gone. I thought to myself, *I hope I see him again.* Then about a week later at the Christmas gathering at the church, I saw him again. We used to get little bags of candies, nuts and apples. He offered me an apple. He said it was to thank me for our kindness. He asked me when I would be finished school. When he heard it would only be another year, he kissed me and told me he would wait for me. It was the most romantic night of my life." She sighed and paused in her memories. "Then we had four boys by the time we were twenty-five. And life was never the same," she laughed.

River felt frozen in place, hanging on her nokomis's every word. She wanted to stay up all night listening, but she knew the night had to eventually end. She hoped there were many more nights like this. Her grandmother's stories were so vivid they came alive in River's mind.

"That was such a good story, Noki, thank you." River slurped the last of her tea.

As her nokomis did the same, she said, "Miigwech. *Miigwech* means 'thank you' in our language, in Anishnaabomowin."

"Well then, miigwech, Nokomis," River said solemnly.

She kissed her nokomis and her dad on the cheek. "Dad, I can't keep my eyes open. Can we hear some of your stories tomorrow?" She stifled her yawn and held her forearm over her mouth.

"Sure, my girl," he responded. "I'll see you bright and early." Then he frowned a bit and added, "I know you're tired, Riv. But can you let your mom know you're okay?"

River nodded her head.

"Goodnight, my sweet girl," her nokomis called up as River went off to her room.

June 25, Later

Nokomis is right, I should call Mom and let her know I am okay. I don't know if I'm ready yet. How can I explain that I don't think I'm even the same person who got on that bus two days ago? I will call Mom in the morning to let her know I'm okay. And she can let Josh and the girls know for now.

The stories of Nokomis and Mishomis are so sweet and romantic. But do they ever show how fast they had to grow up. I can't imagine having four kids by the age of twenty-five. That would be like me and Josh having four kids in the next seven years.

I'm having a hard enough time looking after myself. It's like every day I feel a little bit different. Sometimes it's like I'm outside of myself looking in. But I can see that my thoughts don't always match my feelings, if that makes any sense at all.

I know in my mind that everyone is trying to do the best they can. They are all trying to make the right decisions for me. But then I wonder why I can't make decisions for myself.

My mom talks about leaving our home. Josh talks about school in the fall. Nokomis talks about when she was younger. I feel like they all have their lives all figured out. I don't have a clue who I am or what I am doing.

Hopping on the bus was an impulse. It wasn't really a well-thought-out move. I feel like if I just knew who I was, I could figure all this out so much more easily. It's like I don't really know who I am. Am I a farm girl? Not anymore! Am I a high school student? Not anymore!

Who am I? What am I doing here in Winnipeg when I don't even have a home in Ontario anymore?

CHAPTER 10

He is My Father

River had been with her dad and nokomis for a week. Eric was in his usual routine of waking early and cooking breakfast. He flipped the eggs and stirred the bacon with a fork. River could smell the toast starting to burn, so she popped up the lever on the toaster.

"Good morning, Riv," her dad smiled.

"Morning, Dad. Smells so good." She opened the fridge. "Do you have orange juice?"

"Yep, the kind with no pulp, your favourite."

"Awesome. Thanks."

River slid into the kitchen chair, and fastened her red bandana around her head. She poured herself some juice and buttered the toast.

"Mom said she's going to stay in bed and rest for a while. She had a hard time falling asleep last night." Eric placed the eggs carefully on the plate. "How did you sleep?" he asked.

"I had a hard time falling asleep too. I mean, I was really tired, but my mind was racing like crazy. I love hearing her stories every night. And yours too. I know they are about things that happened a long time ago. But they make me feel like I know myself a bit better or . . . something . . . weird." She shook her head.

Eric just nodded and sipped his coffee.

River thought about the stories her dad and nokomis had been telling her. This was the first time she had even thought about residential schools and the Sixties Scoop as things that had happened to her own family.

"So this might be an awkward breakfast question, Dad," she said. "But how come Noki calls her school, like, just school? She never calls it residential school."

"I'm not sure," her dad replied. "I do know that there are many Elders who don't want to talk about all the bad stuff that happened in those places. The abuse and neglect. They have spent so many years telling their stories, after the Truth and Reconciliation Commission process. Maybe some of them might feel they need a break. They are at the end of their lives, and it almost re-traumatized them to tell their story over and over again. Even though it ended up being healing, it was still very painful. Some just want to spend their final years in the good space, after all their healing work. Don't get me wrong, they'll never forget what happened to them there. They will never forget losing everything, including their sense of spirit."

Sense of spirit. Those words made River's spine tingle.

"Geez, Dad, I've learned so much already."

"A busy start to your summer!"

River and her dad ate in silence. She cleared their plates while her dad put the pan in the sink to soak.

"I don't mean to change the subject, babe," said her dad, wiping his hands. "But I have to head over to help my brother with the siding on his shed. Do you want to come with me? Give you a chance to see your uncle Dean again."

"Uncle Dean is the really smart one, right?"

"Yeah, and I'm the really handsome one!"

River rolled her eyes and smirked. "Okay, yeah, sounds good. Then Noki can have a nice quiet sleep in. Should I just text her? But I don't want to wake her." River looked confused.

"Back in the old days we did something called *writing a note and leaving it on the table*," Eric teased.

River giggled. "Are you sure you aren't the smart one, Dad?"

"Well, yes, I am indeed. Because I knew you would come with me, and I already left her a note. I just have to grab some tools from the garage. I'll meet you in the car."

"Okay, sounds good." River tiptoed to put her sandals on.

She tucked her phone in her back pocket and sat in the driver's side of the car. "I'm driving!" she yelled as her dad walked over from the shed.

"Don't go fast," he warned her as he got in the car beside her. "There are rez cops everywhere. They have nothing to do all day. So they sit with that stupid new speed gun they just got and catch people who are going like three over the speed limit. Drives me nuts!"

"Okay, Dad. I won't speed." River turned the key. "Okay, which one is the brake? And where's the drive forward button?"

"Uhh, are you being serious?"

"Yeah, dead serious. I've never driven a stick before."

"Get out," Eric huffed.

"What, why?"

"Because I am not about to teach you how to drive standard right now. Not when I have to get somewhere in one piece to help someone."

River burst out laughing. "Just kidding, Dad, geez. I grew up on a farm. I can drive a standard tractor with my eyes closed."

She put the car in reverse and backed out of the driveway. She used her mirrors, but didn't actually look behind her. There was never anyone on the road. She shifted into first and popped the clutch, bouncing them down the dirt road. "Oops, just a little bump there, Dad. Just a little rusty, nothing to worry about . . ." She waved to the neighbours and smirked. "Nothing to see here, folks, nothing at all."

Eric laughed with his head down and his chin into his chest. "It's just up here on the left, through two more stop signs."

River pulled into the driveway of a beautiful log cabin with a red tin roof. "Oh, this is a beautiful home, Dad."

"Uncle Dean built it himself. We're just finishing up the shed. And then he will start some small garden beds for fall Indian corn."

"Oohh, I love Indian corn. Mom loves growing it too. Except one year, she thought she would try growing three different kinds. They all ended up weird and small because they cross pollinated."

"Oh, who's the smarty pants now, using big words like cross-pollinated?" Eric teased.

"Hey, Eric. Hey, kiddo!" called a voice as River put the car in park.

Dean, a slight man with a pot belly and a long, black ponytail like Eric's walked over, wiping his hands on his dirty khaki pants. As River was getting out of the car, he surprised her with a tight hug. Her arms were still at her side.

"Hey, Uncle Dean," she said. She struggled for air from inside his squeeze.

River saw her dad give his brother a sharp look. She could tell the warning in his eyes said, *Too soon, Dean.*

"Uh, you guys thirsty?" Dean asked, dropping his hands to his sides. "Want something to drink? A beer?"

Eric slapped the back of his hand against his brother's bicep. "It's ten o'clock in the morning, Dean."

"I know, it's a beautiful day, isn't it?" Dean smiled from ear to ear. "Here, come and see the shed. It's really starting to look good. I just need you guys to hold the siding for me, so I can fasten it on. We should be all done by lunchtime. Will you guys stay for lunch? Sophie is in the house making corn soup and bannock."

Eric looked at River as if to ask her permission. River nodded in agreement.

"Sure, we will stay," said Eric. "River can meet the kids."

"Perfect!" Dean said. "Let's go up and say hi, and then we can get started." River wondered if his cheeks hurt. He had been smiling the whole time.

River's gaze travelled along the stone walkway leading up to the stairs of the log house. The big bay windows reflected the morning sun. Two little children sat on the couch staring at them as they came through the door.

"River, these are your cousins, Sarah and Megan. Say hi, girls." Dean looked at River for her response.

"Hey, girls, how are you? My name is River, and I am so happy to finally meet you." She knelt beside the couch. "Do you like high fives?"

They nodded.

"Here, let's high five then!"

The girls all joined hands in the air.

"Oh, River, look at how all grown up you are." Sophie's country whine came from the kitchen.

"Auntie!" River shuffled across the floor and gave her auntie a big hug.

Sophie squealed. "I can't believe you're really here. It's so nice to see you. Oh, my goodness, your nokomis was just telling me the other day how you are going to be working on your jingle dress and dancing at the powwow. That is just awesome. I've been working on the girls' fancy shawl regalia too. I know they're half breeds, but that's okay. They can dance at the powwow. Like you, right? Maybe you can teach them a few steps!" She let go of River's arms and walked back to the soup, still talking. "And you're going to come and spend some time with us, right? And come and play with the girls — oh, they would love that so much. They have only been out of school for two weeks and they are already driving me nuts — I mean, getting bored."

"Yeah, I'd love to." River smiled politely at the girls.

"Okay, honey. Well, you get out there with your dad and Uncle Dean. I'll see you at lunch. I made your dad's favourite corn soup and bannock."

"Yeah. I've been eating bannock since I got here. I better get out there and work some of it off."

"Oh, nonsense, girl, you have your mother's figure." Sophie smiled too wide. And stirred her soup. Quickly.

AABTOOZII NDAAW

CHAPTER 11

I am a Half Breed

River put the car in park in her grandmother's driveway. Her nokomis waved from the kitchen window. River fake-smiled and waved back. It had been a long day.

She turned to Eric. "Seriously, Dad, that was the strangest visit today with Sophie. What is up with her?"

Eric unwrapped a piece of gum and popped it in his mouth. He chewed as he spoke. "I think she's just really stressed out."

"Let me guess. Is it because Uncle Dean starts drinking the moment he wakes up?" Sarcasm entered River's voice. "Hmm, or could it be that she has her sister's 'half breed kids,' as she puts it, because nobody knows where their mother is? I mean I'm a half breed, but I haven't heard that term since I was teased in grade school." River suddenly realized she was talking to one of the parents who made her a "half breed." "Sorry, Dad. But the way Sophie acted made me so mad!"

Eric threw the crumpled gum wrapper into the console of the car. "No one is perfect, my girl. And your uncle and aunt have their stuff, just like we all do." He looked at her and gently said, "Aren't you here in my car because you have stuff at home too?"

River felt a little ashamed. "I know, I totally shouldn't judge. I just think Sophie shouldn't be saying the girls are half breed, at least not in the presence of the girls. It reminds me of when Nokomis used to talk about my weight in front of me to other adults, shaming me because I was a chubby kid. Geez, Sophie even commented on my weight!"

"I see you have some feelings, Riv. Do you want to talk about what is bothering you? Is it really because Sophie made a joke about the kids being half breeds?"

River paused to work through her own thoughts. "Dad, where's Sophie's sister?"

"No one knows, my girl. They aren't sure if she took off because it just got to be too much for her. Or if she actually might be missing. She does this from time to time, takes off to be alone. She's a troubled soul. They reported her missing just in case."

"I can't believe this, Dad. This is so crazy. So Sophie will just keep the kids until she shows up? Even if she never does?"

"Yep."

"Why?" River rolled down her window. A warm breeze dried the beads of sweat trickling down her cheek.

"Why what?" Eric asked.

"Why is it like this? Why are there so many broken families on the rez? And so many people who drink their problems away? Seriously, Dad, why?"

"Oh, my girl, there are so many reasons. And it's not just on the rez. It happens regardless of race. Wanna talk about it over tea tonight?"

"I know that it's not just here. But, yeah, I'd like to know what you think."

"I think your nokomis might have a softer perspective too," Eric added.

"Okay," River agreed.

"Hey, thanks for your help today, kiddo. I can tell your mama did a good job raising you on that farm. I can tell you are a hard worker."

At the thought of the farm, River looked away so he wouldn't see the start of tears.

"And maybe we can talk about that tonight too, hey?"

"Mm-hmm," River mumbled.

"I'm going in for a nice cold lemonade. Want me to bring you some?"

River could only nod. She looked in the mirror and dried her eyes as her dad disappeared into the house.

He returned with lemons and ice clinking in glass tumblers. He passed River her glass through the car window.

"I know it might be weird timing to ask you this. But I was also wondering if you wanted to head into Winnipeg with me next week. There's a band playing, and I would love to go see them. I might bring my guitar and play too. There's an open mic jam session."

"Um . . . don't I have to be nineteen to get into a bar?" River sipped her lemonade and made a sour face.

"Not in Manitoba. You only have to be eighteen. Rules are a little different here." He winked and mimed toasting her with his glass.

"Yeah and the stop lights are weird too!" River laughed. "Sure! What do I wear? I've never been to a bar before. Is it like fancy? Or can I just wear my jeans and T-shirt?"

"You can wear whatever you like. But, yeah, jeans and a T-shirt are fine."

"Okay." River knew her dad was trying to change the subject by asking her to go out. But she thought she'd give it one more try. "But, Dad, can you give me a short answer? Why are the things the way they are on the rez?"

"You don't give up, eh? Persistent like your mom too, I see."

River stared.

"Okay, okay, short answer, my girl. Residential schools. And the intergenerational effects."

"I don't even know what that means. And how can the residential schools be the cause of so many different problems? How? I don't get it."

"That would make my short answer a long one, my girl."

"I'm listening."

"I said we can talk about it tonight."

"DAD!"

Eric leaned on the hood of the car. "Fine. People who went to residential school, or people from the Sixties Scoop, they still have a hard time with 'normal' family stuff. They didn't grow up with a strong loving family. They suffered abuse. Lots of it. People died. And it doesn't just affect them. It affects the whole family. All of their kids. Their grandkids. I think that maybe you still suffer from your grandmother's experience at residential school, or mine. I was not able to provide a stable loving home for you or your mother. And that's because of what I went through. It's hard to create a stable family without self-compassion. And it's hard to have self-compassion when you come out of a situation like we did."

"Oh, Dad . . ." River put her glass down. "I'm sorry. I shouldn't have kept bugging you. It's just that I don't know what to say or do a lot of the time. I feel like it's my fault I don't understand any of this."

Eric's eyes met hers. She could see him fighting through the painful memories. "Don't be sorry, sweetie. And don't feel you need to carry that shame. It's not yours to carry. It's not your fault."

"I didn't know you went to residential school, Dad. Mom never told me that."

"I don't think she even knew. I couldn't talk about it back then. It's taken me a long time to get to the point where I can. I was thinking last night, though. It's probably time you heard the truth from me. You know, about why I wasn't around when you were small."

Eric sipped the last of his lemonade. He set the glass down on the hood of the car and wiped his goatee with his hands. "Can you at least get out of the car now?"

River opened the car door. Eric took her hand and led her out to sit on the steps.

"River, the truth is that I never stopped loving your mom. Your mom and I split up because I was making her miserable. Not having a steady job. Being out all night, chasing my music career. That's hard on a woman with a small child. But now I wonder if it was just as much about trying to avoid bringing you both into my damage. Me not being around was because of me. It was all me, and not your mother. I just want you to know that."

River hung her head. She sat with her hands clasped behind her neck.

Eric went on sharing his thoughts. River could tell it wasn't easy for him. It wasn't easy for her. But she thought that maybe he needed to say it as much as she needed to hear it.

Her dad shared how he had begged her mom to take him back, but she wouldn't. She wasn't going to let him just walk in and out of her life. In and out of River's life. He told her how his heart ached when he left his daughter. Like a heavy rock sinking to the bottom of the lake.

"Residential school made it hard for me to trust people," Eric said. "It was hard for me to let anyone get close, let alone stay close. Hell, maybe that's why all my relationships never worked out. Not just the one with your mom. Maybe it's why I live with your nokomis instead of having my own family. It was hard for me to even stay in one town for very long. I think I was running from the shame and deep feelings I couldn't face."

As River started to cry, Eric said softly, "So to get back to your first question. Maybe that's what Sophie's sister was going through too. She didn't go to residential school. But she still had to deal with the pain of her parents. You know, almost every parent here on the rez is of that generation."

"I had no idea, Dad," River sniffled.

"Oh, River, I didn't mean to upset you. I just . . . I thought maybe it was time to tell you this, and . . ."

"No, it's okay. I wanted to hear this. I just had no idea how to bring it up, or when a good time to bring it up would be. It's like . . . I mean . . . um . . . I think, Dad, I always felt like you didn't love me. I thought if you loved me then you and Mom would try to make it work. I mean, as I grew up I started to get that it's not that easy. I know it doesn't work like that. I think I have just always been yearning for your love."

"Oh, my sweet River, I am so sorry you have held on to that thought all this time."

Eric stood and stepped back from the step to look his daughter in the eyes. "I always hoped you knew how much I loved you. But it was hard when we only spent a short time together each summer. Now we are ready to talk about these things, I want us to heal. I know you will never forget your childhood. But I really do hope we can heal from the past."

River smiled. "We really nailed this bonding thing, didn't we?"

Eric nodded in agreement and smiled back.

River entered the house quietly. She kissed her nokomis on the cheek and told her she would be down after she freshened up a bit. Her nokomis took in the traces of tears on River's face. River felt those kind eyes on her as she walked upstairs.

July 2

So I missed our Canada Day plans with my friends back home.

I can't believe how drained I feel. I feel like I have been at a funeral for the past week. I feel happy, then sad. Then angry and frustrated and scared. All at the same time. How do people handle adulting? God, no wonder people drink. I feel like I need a break. I thought coming out here was going to be a break. It just turns out there's even more stuff to process.

How is Auntie Sophie dealing? Looks like she's not. I wonder if we'll ever know where Sophie's sister is. This is serious, her missing when Indigenous women and girls are being found dead. And people are just acting like it's normal. Those poor girls. Imagine never knowing when your mom is going to be around.

Dad's story was super emotional and crazy. I have never heard my dad talk like that. I wonder what would have happened if he ever talked to Mom like that. I mean, I can see why my mom fell in love with him. Oh, that sounded too weird. I just mean, he's not about the judging or anything. And he is handsome, with his long braid. But he isn't really the perfect man that I thought he was. Or the perfect father I always dreamed of having.

My grandmother though, I can't believe what that woman

has been through. What all of them have been through. I knew all this stuff happened, but it's never hit me this hard before. I can't imagine going to school and starving and watching your friends die. Being beaten for speaking your language and suffering abuse. I mean, just being away from home for so long and to be so little. Oh my gosh, I would have just died of heartbreak, missing Mom.

I wonder how they could even be happy after going through something like that? How do you move on with your life? And then imagine having to worry about your kids going to residential school too, when you know exactly what happens there. I keep feeling this pukey feeling. It feels like I just can't handle these thoughts.

I don't know how Noki made it through. I don't know if I could have survived it and still have a generous heart. Maybe I'll ask her how she did it. If she made it through all that, I feel like I should be able to make it through anything. My life is a bowl of peaches compared to hers when she was my age.

CHAPTER 12

It is a Nice Evening

River could hear her dad calling up the stairs. It was a perfect July evening — hot, but not humid like it would be in Ontario. River decided to wear a khaki skirt and a burgundy tank top with lace at the bottom. She slid her feet into her favourite flip flops.

River saw her dad smile as he watched her tap each toe carefully down the stairs. He was in his favourite worn out red T-shirt with a headdress on it, and his khaki shorts with lots of pockets. His hair was pulled back into a ponytail. He had on white socks and sandals.

"Hey, we match!" he said.

River smirked at his socks and sandals. "No, Dad. We don't. Burgundy and red don't match. They don't contrast well either. It's okay, though. It just means we can't sit near each other all night."

Eric scrunched his eyebrows and raised his hands out to his side as he shrugged. "Why not? You don't want to be seen with your old daddy at the bar?"

"Dad, don't say 'old daddy' out loud. Ever. Again. You're not my daddy. Well, like, you are, but you're not, like, my DADDY, daddy . . . See what I'm sayin'?"

"Nope. Don't know and don't care right now. I'm super pumped for this band. You wanna drive to Winnipeg? Just one straight road. Then I can drive in the city."

"Sure." River caught the keys mid-air with her right hand. "Let's do this!"

When they reached the city limits, River pulled over and let Eric drive. She pushed the seat back to make room for him before she got out and switched sides.

They decided to visit an art gallery he used to take her to when she was small. As they stepped through the door, River's eyes were filled with the sight of red dresses hanging from the ceiling.

What is this? River wondered. She wasn't sure why she had such a strong reaction to the dresses. So she went to view the artist's statement. The art installation was created to bring awareness to the hundreds of missing and murdered Indigenous women and girls. There was tablet that cycled pictures of the missing women, with their names and *Missing Since* dates in bold text. River felt a chill that had nothing to do with the air conditioning.

Eric respected River's silence as they left the gallery and walked down to the Grand Forks. They walked by the stage where the Winnipeg Folk Festival was held. Eric had talked about playing there many times. They walked into the market and ordered some maple fudge, another favourite memory from when River was a little girl. Eric took River to the playground where she broke her toe when she was ten. He took her to the bookstore where he bought the first book he had ever given her when she was eight. They decided on the Old Spaghetti Factory for dinner and ended their evening out on the town with ice cream. Their bellies and hearts were full.

As the sun went down, they made their way into the bar. The bouncer at the door put his hand up in front of River and asked for her ID. He read her Ontario licence, glanced at her and looked back down at the licence. He looked at Eric sternly.

Eric piped up, "She's my daughter visiting from Ontario."

The bouncer replied, "Yeah, buddy, I don't normally judge. But we gotta keep girls safe these days, you know."

Eric responded, "Yes, man. Yes, we do."

The bouncer held the door open, and they made their way inside. The floor was black and dirty, and the place was still mostly empty. The techs were working on sound checks and the girl at the door asked them for a six dollar cover charge. The girl stamped their hands with invisible ink. River wondered how they could check for re-entry on a stamp you couldn't see. Her dad laughed at her questioning look and explained that the stamp was visible under a black light lamp.

They walked toward the left side of the bar. Eric ordered a Tom Collins for himself and a Diet Coke for River. They took a seat in the very back, up the ramp and in a booth. There were mirrors all along the wall. River caught a glimpse of herself with her dad in a bar, and thought to herself, *Weird.*

Eric passed her the Diet Coke and she took a sip. As they settled in, River looked up at every person who passed their table. She had never seen so many Indigenous people in a bar before. Maybe because she had never been in a bar before. She was also surprised how many of them were half in the bag when they arrived. She watched a large woman slurring her words as she scolded her very skinny boyfriend for looking at another woman just ten minutes into their evening.

All River's friends at home sneaked the odd drink, like a cold beer in the summer. But River never did. She wondered if she would feel less out of place if she had a drink with alcohol in it.

"Do you think I could try an actual drink, Dad?" she asked.

"Wow, not shy about that one, eh?" smiled Eric. "Sure, I guess.

If you're old enough to be here, you're old enough to drink. Just don't tell your mother."

"Right." River nodded slowly. After all, it was all legal here.

"What would you like?" he asked.

River gave a blank stare.

"You have no idea, do you, babe?"

She shook her head no.

"Okay, how about a rum and coke. Just don't drink anything else all night."

"Why?"

"Don't mix your booze. Like, if you're drinking rum, don't drink beer. Or if you drink beer, don't drink wine. It will make you too sick. Geez, didn't your mother tell you any of this?"

"Nope. Mom doesn't talk to me about drinking. I feel like she thinks if she doesn't talk about it, I won't do it. I don't know. I don't drink anyway. This will be my first time."

"Christ." Eric's voice turned suddenly sober.

"What?" River was surprised at her dad's tone.

"Nothing, I just think parents should be talking to kids about things like that." He shrugged. "Otherwise, how will you know?"

Suddenly, River was distracted by a rowdy crowd entering the bar.

"Ah, there they are," Eric said. He waved his friends over and pulled up some chairs at their table. "I'll get our drinks while I'm up. I'll get you a double."

River wasn't sure what that meant. But she nodded with a smile and tapped her toes to the music.

KWE GII GIISHKWEBII

CHAPTER 13

The Lady Got Drunk

The opening band strutted across the mini stage. The thirty or so people in the bar clapped and whistled. There was a dance floor where two women, wearing tight black clothes and looked about the same age as River's parents, started dancing to the upbeat blues song. River smiled at them. She loved how they were dancing like nobody was watching. She wished she could do that. But she was too shy to dance in front of everyone.

By the time the headliner took the stage, River was feeling relaxed and happy. The man with a great smile and ponytail started his first set playing the blues on his electric cigar-box guitar. By the time his girlfriend joined him on stage, even more people had arrived at the bar, and the place lit up. Her raspy voice made the audience scream.

River looked over at her dad, who was bopping his head to the music. He was clearly enjoying himself. She saw him sneak in a little air guitar once or twice, in addition to the toe tapping. He had three empty glasses in front of him. She smiled and chugged the rest of her double rum and coke.

Three more men pulled battered chairs up to their table. River shuffled over a little and instantly made eye contact with the youngest. He was a little older than she was, with short, black hair. His T-shirt was tight in all the right places, so she could tell he worked out. His friend, a little heavier, a little older, had a huge curly mane. He called himself Motley Cree, which made people laugh hysterically. River didn't really get it, but she smiled and laughed anyway. The third guy was fairly stocky, with a buzz cut. They didn't talk much, but they seemed to enjoy the music.

"River, these are my friends from way back," Eric said. He gestured at the two older guys. "This is Tony and Allan, and this is . . ." Eric clearly didn't know the younger guy's name.

The gorgeous man put his hand out to shake River's. "Russell," he said.

"Hi, I'm Russell," River blurted. "Oh my god, I mean, I'm River." She could feel her face turn fifty shades of red. She turned her head and looked at the wall. She tried to compose herself, biting her bottom lip, before she turned back to face him.

"Nice to meet you, River." Russell's eyes sparkled.

"Nice to meet you too," River squeaked. She stuck out her hand awkwardly to shake his.

He grabbed her hand as if he was about to drop to one knee and ask for it in marriage. "Uh . . . so you wanna dance?"

River's eyes went wide. She thought of Josh. They danced together all the time. In his basement, or in the barn, or in the meadow. But this would be dancing in a bar with a guy she had met just that second.

River didn't know how long she stared at Russell before she blurted out, "Yep!" She grabbed his other hand and led him to the dance floor. She didn't have a clue where the spark of confidence came from, but she went with it. *It might be the drink*, she thought.

She didn't really know how to dance to blues music. But she bopped around, trying to appear carefree. *Any guy would love to be next to a carefree kind of girl, right?* she thought.

They didn't talk at all, but by the fourth song, they were dripping in sweat. Russell gestured to the bar and asked her if she wanted another. She remembered what her dad said and asked for a rum and coke. From his chair, her dad gave her a little wave. She could see he was delighted to see her let loose.

Russell was back quickly with a drink. "I made it a double," he said as he handed it to her, along with a slip of paper with something written on it. He smiled. "That's my number. I want to see you again."

For a moment she was taken aback. *This guy is way too smooth*, she thought. But the rational moment didn't last long. "Um, okay." She grinned ear to ear. She put the piece of paper in her pocket and held up her drink to clink the glass against his bottle of beer.

Her eyes never left his as she chugged her drink.

Geez, that's strong, she thought as she felt her lips go too numb to speak. She wondered what her mother would think. She wondered what Josh would think.

"What are you doing tonight?" Russell whispered in her ear as they danced.

"Umm . . . depends," she whispered back.

"Well, there's a party at my best friend's house. I'm staying with him for a few weeks. You should come." He stepped back so his face was about a foot from hers. He didn't take his eyes from hers as he mouthed the words of the song to her.

"I'll have to ask my dad," River said. "Only because he's driving me, though. I don't have to ask his permission or anything. I just don't have a car. Here. I mean, I don't have a car here. And I'm not sure when I'm going to stop acting like a spaz. Are you sure you want me to go with you?"

"It's okay if you act like a spaz," said Russell with a smile. "I know where it's coming from. I feel it too."

"You do?" Her tummy fluttered.

"Yep." He grabbed her by the waist and pulled her body close to his. He danced from side to side to the rhythm of the blues, singing in her ear.

River laughed, throwing her head back. She wrapped her arms around his neck, following his lead.

A few songs later, she needed a rest. She went back to the table and sat down beside her dad. She tried not to appear too drunk.

"Having fun, babe?" Eric asked.

"Heck yeah!" River said far too loudly. "Dad, is it okay if I go to an after party with these guys?"

She saw that there were a couple more empty glasses in front of him. But it didn't occur to her that he was not in the clearest frame of mind when he said, "Yeah, these are decent guys. Sure!"

As her father spoke, River's thoughts drifted. She could see his lips moving, but his words seemed to linger in the air. She thought about how her friends would be freaking out right now. She thought about Josh only for a moment. Then she cleared her throat and shoved the image of Josh's face deep inside. She wanted to feel free. Free from the feelings she wasn't used to. Free from the confusion she had felt since the summer started. Free from the pain that was masked by the rum. She kissed her dad on the cheek and left the bar with Russell.

CHAPTER 14

I am Afraid

River hopped into the back of the white two-door Honda Civic, Russell led her to. She didn't have a clue who was driving, where they were going or what time it was. She didn't care. She wanted to leave all of her pain behind her and have the night of her life. Of her *new* life.

The driver pulled into an alley behind a row of houses. The garage door opened by remote and the car fit perfectly inside. They got out and stumbled up the wooden stairs. Then through a back door into a kitchen. In the narrow house the air was stifling hot and smoky from cigarettes. Music blared from the living room. There were pockets of people in every room, and everyone seemed to be wearing black.

River had a sudden sense of unease. She let Russell know she was going to step into the washroom. She needed a moment to gather herself. With a little splash, she cooled her face with water and looked for a hand towel. She had no luck, so she patted her face dry with the bottom of her T-shirt. She looked in the mirror and opened her eyes wide as she felt for the door knob.

River opened the bathroom door and looked out. She couldn't quite make out what she was seeing. She wasn't sure if it was because it was too dark . . . or just too odd. Maybe her brain just couldn't process what she was seeing. The woman in the room across the hall was squatting with her pants down. Urine trickled onto the floor and into the hall. River stepped over it, holding herself up against the wall with the palms of her hands.

She walked through the living room, looking for Russell. She stopped as she noticed two small children lying on a couch. They were watching TV, wearing only diapers and drinking from a bottle of milk.

Whoa, River thought. *It's way too late for those little kids to be awake.* She walked over and put a blanket on them. Their eyes blinked up at her. River noticed someone on the other couch, but she was passed out.

What kind of party is this? she wondered. *Where the hell am I?*

River's head spun a little as she made her way back to the kitchen. There she found Russell standing with a group of guys. They were tough looking, like rappers, and wore red bandanas.

River placed her hand on Russell's hip. She fought to stay upright. Russell placed his hand on the small of her back. "You okay?" he asked in her ear.

"Yeah, I think I just had a little too much to drink. It's catching up with me."

"Wanna go upstairs and lie down for a bit?" River could feel a suspicious look cross her face as she processed his offer. He raised both hands in the air as if he was being searched by police. "I swear. Nothing else. I just want to make sure you are okay."

"Sorry, Russell. I know we just got here. I just, I just don't feel well."

"It's totally fine. C'mon, I'll take you up."

He twined his fingers with hers and led her up the stairs. She lay on her side on the bed in an empty bedroom and brought her knees to her chest.

Russell gave her an extra pillow and turned on a fan. "This is the room where I'm staying. I'll come up and check on you in twenty minutes or so. Just text me if you need me."

"Okay," she managed to say. Even lying down, she had to try to maintain her balance as a wave of nausea rolled through her. She reached into her pocket to find the piece of paper Russell had given her at the bar. She programmed his number into her phone just before her eyes closed. Her cell phone slid from her hand to the bed.

It couldn't have been very long before she heard the door knob turn and the floor creak. Looking up from the bed, she saw two girls hunched over the dresser. One of the girls was slicing something on top of the dresser with a bank card. The other girl was rolling up a twenty-dollar bill. River turned her back to them, pretending to sleep.

"I see you, River." The first girl laughed.

"Want some? It will help you stay awake," the second girl offered.

"No, I'm good. Thanks," River groaned. As she ran her hand across the bed for her phone, she wondered, *How do they know my name?*

Russell: Hey River, you doing okay?
River: Can you come upstairs?
Russell: Already? lol
River: No, seriously. I'm scared.
Russell: Be right up.

Russell opened the door with his foot. He scanned the bedroom.

"Hey, Russ!" one of the girls squealed.

"What are you doing in here?" Russell scolded. "Upstairs is always off limits. You two know that." He held the door open for them until they left. River could hear their cackling echo down the hallway.

Russell closed the door softly. "Sorry about that, River. They know better."

"Who are they?" she whispered.

"They're Alvin's girls," he answered.

"Like Alvin and the Chipmunks?" River smirked.

"Oh, so you're beautiful *and* funny, eh?"

"Maybe . . . No, but really, who's Alvin? And what do you mean, they're his girls?"

"Alvin's the leader of the Northern Rebels. Nothing to worry about, though. You're safe with me. He's not a pimp or anything. He just has, well, girls."

"What's the Northern Rebels?"

"Seriously?"

"Yeah, seriously."

"Um, the largest Native gang in Manitoba?"

"What the hell? Where are we? Who *are* you?"

"Umm. We're in Winnipeg, at my best friend's house. And I'm Russell."

"Okay, like I know all that. But what part of the city are we in?"

"The North End."

So this is the infamous North End, she thought. Her dad had warned her. Her mom had warned her. "Stay away from the North End," they said. It was a place where dark things happened. River knew it was best to stay on the other side of town. The safer side, if there was such a thing.

"I think I need to go home," River said. She tried to sit up.

"River, you're not going anywhere tonight. It's three a.m. I'll take you home in the morning. You want to come back downstairs? Or do you want to go back to sleep? Here, I'll get you some water." Russell leaned over and grabbed an unopened water bottle from beside the bed. He held it in front of her.

"Thank you. I think I'll just sleep this off. I had no idea I was in the North End."

As she sipped the water, her mind cleared enough for one thing to fall into the place. "Oh my god, Russell. Are you in a gang?" River sat up and backed up against the headboard like an animal in the back of a cage.

Russell laughed. "Is that what you think?"

"Just answer the question," she demanded.

"No, I'm not part of a gang. These guys and gals are like my family, though. I'm safe, and you're safe. That's all you need to know."

River whispered with fear in her voice, "I'm so stupid. This is how girls go missing, isn't it? I shouldn't have come here with you. I don't even know you."

"Calm down, River. It's okay, I swear. Nobody is going missing. Get some rest. You'll be fine. Just don't go downstairs and start anything."

"Russell?"

"Yes, River?"

"Please don't kill me in my sleep," she whispered.

"Oh my god. All right. I won't kill you in your sleep." He held his hand out to ease her back until she was lying down. He fluffed her pillow and tucked her in.

"Thanks, Russell."

"No problem. Get some rest. I'll see you in the morning."

"Wait."

"What now?" he whined. But there was a smile on his face.

"Will you just stay here with me? Just sleep beside me. I'm totally scared. But I'm so tired, I need to sleep."

"Oh, so you're needy!"

"Needy and scared are not the same thing!"

"Fine. Move over."

Russell plopped down beside her. He was snoring within thirty seconds.

The last image in River's mind was Josh's face. She squeezed her eyes tightly as if to hold it there as she drifted off to sleep.

CHAPTER 15

I Look at Him Behind Me

Light pierced a break in the sheets nailed to the top and edges of the window. It shot into River's eyes. She rubbed her cheek to make sure there was no drool. She was still in Russell's arms.

River looked around the room. She saw the dresser, and remembered what she had seen. The word *cocaine* wasn't a part of her vocabulary. Except for maybe in grade six when the police came to the school to scare the kids into not doing drugs.

She remembered her conversation with Russell clearly. She lay still, unsure of her next move. She couldn't just leave. She had no idea where she was. She had no idea where her wallet was. Her phone was on six percent.

Shit, she mouthed to herself.

She rolled over. Russell's eyes were still closed. No drool, and he was not snoring. He looked like the guy in the *Twilight* movies. The handsome guy who turned into a werewolf. Like that guy, he had perfectly tanned skin. Perfect eyebrows, a perfect nose. But he smelled delicious, not like a wolf, even through the smell of beer.

River wondered why Russell was interested in her, of all the girls in the bar. She thought about Josh and wondered how she could be attracted to two people who were so different. Both were sweet and funny, but in completely different ways.

Her eyes caught on where Russell's T-shirt was raised a little above his waist. His eyes opened, and she knew she was caught staring at him.

Russell smiled. "Checking me out as soon as you wake up. Ever good, you!"

"Um . . . no," she shook her head.

"Don't lie." He sat up and leaned back on one arm. "How did you sleep?

Butterflies danced in her tummy. "Okay, except for your snoring."

"Never mind, liar. You were the one sawing logs all night."

"I'm sorry I was a spaz last night. I've just never been, like, in this kind of place. I've never hung out with this kind of people before. I grew up on a farm in southern Ontario. I still live on a farm. Well, not for long. But, Russell, I've never even had a drink before. I was totally freaked out."

Russell sat all the way up. "What do you mean, 'this kind of people'? They're just people, like you and me, River. You're no better than they are."

"No, no, I didn't mean that. I just mean I've never partied in my life. Like, I'm seriously so boring. I ride my horse, hang out with my friends and do homework. And that's it."

"Oh, so you're a college girl and you have horses?"

"Uhh . . . I just finished high school." River winced.

"Pardon?"

"What?" Her eyes were wide.

"Damn, girl, I thought you were in your twenties!" His voice was high.

"Does that change things?"

"Uhhh . . . well . . . I just wasn't expecting you to be so young, that's all."

"Yeah, well it was my first time in a bar."

"Yeah, me too," Russell joked.

River punched his bicep. "Yeah, right!"

"Ouch! Damn, girl. I'm a lover, not a fighter."

River smiled. She flexed both arms in the air and kissed her own biceps.

"C'mon," said Russell. "I'll borrow my cousin's car. We can go get some breakfast. And then I'll take you home."

"Sounds good," she agreed. She folded the log cabin quilt and laid it at the foot of the bed. "Where will we go for breakfast?"

"Don't worry, I'll take you somewhere nice," he laughed.

It was a short drive to the diner. Russell parked and opened the car door for River. He held the diner door open too, and pulled out her chair. He took a menu from the neat stack beside the ketchup, salt and pepper and handed it to her.

She accepted with a suspicious eye. "You know, my dad says when something is too good to be true, it's usually not real."

"Ouch, that's heavy for breakfast talk, don't ya think?" Russell responded.

"Oh, uh, sorry. I just mean, why are you being so nice to me? I feel like this totally out-of-it girl. I don't even know what I'm doing here." Then she blurted, "Russell, I have a boyfriend back home."

"Okay, wow. That's not what I was expecting to hear."

He pretended to read the menu.

She pretended to read the menu.

"What do you want me to say?" Russell said without looking up.

"I don't know. That's the whole problem. I have no idea what I am even doing here. I'm, like, really sorry. Can you take me home? I'm not very hungry anyway. I feel sick."

"Uh . . . sure." Russell stood up and ordered a coffee to go. Once again, he held the diner door and the car door for her. They drove in silence, and she drifted to sleep watching the prairies dance.

* * *

"River . . . wake up . . . we're here. You're home." Russell jiggled her seatbelt.

"Oh my god, my head is pounding." River covered her eyes with the fold in her arm.

"Well, c'mon. Let's get you inside and you can sleep it off."

As Russell helped her up to the porch, Eric met them at the door.

"Thanks for bringing her home in one piece, Russell!" Eric said loudly. River winced.

"No problem, Eric," said Russell in a quieter voice. "We had a blast. But she's ready for some more sleep, I think."

"Here, let me help you, Riv," offered Eric. "Will I see you at the powwow in a few weeks, Russell?" he asked.

"Yeah, I'll be there," he said. But River could hear that Russell sounded unsure.

"Okay, see you then!" Eric smiled.

"Thank you, Dad," River muttered.

"Yeah, no problem, kiddo," he mumbled.

Russell shook his head as he walked down the stairs back to his car. River watched him drive away before going in the house.

In that moment, she couldn't understand why she slept over at some stranger's house with someone she had just met. Was it the booze that made her do that? She also wondered why her dad let her go. She made her way up to her room and pulled her journal from the nightstand drawer.

July 10

Oh man, it's not even the middle of July. I feel like I have been away from home for months.

I think I officially have my first hangover. What a night. I feel like I am living someone else's life. All I know is that one day, I am at home on the farm, and three weeks later I'm in the North End of Winnipeg with some guy I don't even know.

I'm pretty sure I saw people doing cocaine. I'm also fairly certain that I saw a woman peeing on the floor. How drunk do you have to be to do that?

I also just remembered that I saw a really young girl passed out on a couch with foam around her mouth. She was on the other couch, not the couch with the babies that were still up at two a.m. Maybe she was the babysitter? Where was their mom? And why do I keep having to ask that question? All I know is that I never had to ask that about my mom.

On the other hand, I don't know how I'd answer if my mom asked me about what I was doing. I slept on the same bed as a guy. Nothing actually happened. But if it was the other way around and Josh got drunk and stayed over with another girl, I would be really upset.

What am I doing? It's like watching my own train wreck. I don't drink, and here I am. Hungover.

This is not who I want to be. This is not who I am.

CHAPTER 16

Sun Appearing From the Sky

"How was your night, my girl?" River's nokomis asked.

"It was pretty crazy, Noki. Not what I expected at all. Parties at home on the farm are seriously low key. Like, we sit around in chairs at a bonfire and people play guitars and sing. Some people drink, but not many. And it's never crazy. I've never seen a party like the one last night *ever* in my life. Way different, that's for sure."

"Mm-hmm." She hummed in an all-knowing kind of way. "And you were in the North End?"

"Mm-hmm," River repeated. It was the first time River felt awkward around her nokomis. But the lecture River was expecting never came.

"Well, I'm glad you're home," was all she said. "And I'm glad you're safe. I don't know what your dad was thinking, letting you go from the bar."

"I was thinking she was with decent guys," Eric piped up from the other room. "I knew she would be okay, Mom."

"What he doesn't know is how mothers worry about their babies," said Grace pointedly to River. "I was worried about you."

That's it? thought River. She thought about what her mom would have had to say about her dad taking her to a bar. Buying her a drink. Letting her go off who-knows-where with a guy she just met. And Grace wasn't calling her son on it. River wondered how she would have turned out if she was raised with no rules at all.

River called out to the other room. "Where did you stay, Dad?"

"Oh, I stayed at Susan's."

"Who's Susan?" River asked, raising her eyebrows.

"Um. Our cousin."

"Oh!" River laughed. Not wanting to slip back into awkward silence, River blurted out, "But seriously, Nokomis, Dad. I think I need help."

"What do you mean?" Grace asked. Eric walked into the room and sat on the couch beside her.

"I need to talk to someone. Noki, you were mentioning that there was a place where youth can go in the city? I know I can talk to both of you. But I feel like I have so many questions, and so many things to figure out. I don't even know where to start. I haven't really talked to anyone from back home since I've been here. And we haven't talked about anything that's going on at home. I thought that last night I could just be free from my mind for one night. And now it's all just crashing down on me. It's too much."

"I understand, my girl." Grace went into the other room. She came back with her little blue phone book. It had sticky notes hanging off each edge. "It's time, River. It's time for you to see an Elder. To hear the stories of some other people closer to your own age."

Grace looked through her book to find a phone number. She wrote the number down on a piece of paper and passed it to River. "The youth circles are on Saturday nights, River. There's one tonight you can go to. They have them on Saturday nights on purpose. To give youth another option."

"Okay," River nodded. "Dad, can you take me?"

"Of course I will, my girl," Eric agreed.

"Thanks, Dad. I'm just gonna go chill outside for a bit. I think it's time I called home."

"Sounds good," Eric said. The smile on his face was concerned, but warm.

River sat in the wooden chair on her nokomis's front porch and sent her friends a group text.

River: Hey Charlie, Hey Jazz. How are u guys?

Charlie instantly responded.

Charlie: ARE YOU OKAY? I have been waiting every day for you to text.

River: Long story. I'm ok. You could have texted me too!

Charlie: Your mom and Josh said not to!

River: Really? Why?

Charlie: So we don't stress you out.

Jasmine: Josh is worried SICK about you. Can you at least just call him once?

River: Yes, I will. Just wanted to tell you guys I'm ok.

Charlie: Thanks Riv. We love you.

River: Love you both.

Charlie: Xoxoxo

Jasmine: Xoxoxoxo <3

* * *

"Hello?" Josh picked up on the first ring.

"Hey, it's me."

"Are you okay?"

"Not really."

"Are you safe?"

"Yeah, I'm totally safe. I'm at my dad's in Winnipeg."

"Yeah, your mom told us. She's really worried you know."

"Oh, is that why she hasn't called?"

"Riv, would you have talked to her anyway?"

"No."

"Exactly. She was trying to give you space. She knew you would come around when you were ready."

"Yeah, well, I'm not really ready yet."

"I'm glad you called me. I'm really glad you called. I love you, River, and you need to know that. I'm here for you. Whatever you need."

River couldn't help it. She began to sob. How could she have done what she did when he was being so nice to her, so caring? "Thank you. I love you too, Josh."

"Can I call you?"

"Yes, of course. You can call me anytime. Just remember there's an hour time difference. I'm heading into Winnipeg tonight for a sharing circle at the youth centre."

"What's a sharing circle?"

"I think it's like a talking circle for youth, and it's led by an Elder. They help young people work stuff out, in a cultural way, I think."

"That's good. I'm glad you're going."

"Mm-hmm," she agreed.

"Can you tell me what you need to work out?"

She said nothing.

Josh prompted. "I know there is all the stuff with your mom and moving. But is there anything else you need to talk about, Riv?"

"Yeah, but not right now. Not yet. Maybe after the circle tonight. I feel like my head is spinning in the clouds right now."

"Please know you can call me anytime. Day or night. I love you."

River was silent. She was used to talking with Josh about

everything about her life back home. But how could she begin to tell him about everything she was feeling now? All the things she had learned. All the things that were confusing her.

"I love you too, Josh. Thank you. We will talk soon, okay?" she sniffled.

"Okay, my love."

"Bye, Josh."

"Bye, Riv."

River hung up the phone. She paused and took a deep breath.

She refused to think about the unease in her stomach. It seemed to be attached to the image of Russell's face. She thought about how supportive Josh had always been. How could she possibly be attracted to someone else, when she had an awesome boyfriend? She couldn't figure it out. Was she attracted to Russell because he took an interest in her? Or was it because he was attractive in a different way, like no other man she had ever seen or talked to before? And how much of it was because of the ways River herself was changing?

She walked down the stairs to a little clearing under a tree in the yard. She lay on her back and looked up at the sky, wiping her eyes. She watched the fluffy white clouds change form, from a thunderbird, to a sweat lodge, to a cedar tree and then to a whale. Her favourite thing to look at was the crystal-clear blue sky, touching the tips of the green leaves on the trees. The sun peeked through a cloud and she closed her eyes. Before she knew it she was asleep.

CHAPTER 17

I am Relating

River walked down the stairs into the church basement. The strong summer wind blew the door open. She walked through several doorways and finally into a room. A guy and three girls, all around her age, were unstacking old wooden chairs and placing them in a circle.

"Ahniin!" the guy said, smiling ear to ear. "I'm Geoff."

"Hi," River responded quietly.

"You're early." That was the girl with large beaded hoop earrings. "My name is Mel. Wanna help us with the chairs?"

"Sure, yeah, no problem."

People started wandering through the doorway, maybe four or five at a time. In no time at all, the circle was full of teenagers. Most of them had been there before, she could tell. They walked right in and sat down as if they had done it a hundred times before. Everyone seemed comfortable around one another.

"Okay, peeps, we're gonna start," an elderly woman began. She didn't introduce herself.

This must be Elaine, Noki's friend, River thought.

Elaine picked up a bag from beneath her chair. She pulled out a shiny seashell and placed some sage inside. She used matches to light the medicine and passed the bowl to Mel, who was sitting on her left. Mel held the shell for Elaine to smudge herself. Elaine wafted the smoke rising from the bowl up over her head and body. She smudged her ears, her eyes, her mouth and her heart. Mel handed the shell back to Elaine and took her turn smudging. Elaine walked around the circle, offering the smudge to each person. One by one, they each smudged themselves, clearing their minds and opening their hearts. When it was River's turn, her hands were shaky.

Elaine talked about the smudging and the sage. How the sage came from the earth. How it was a woman's medicine. She reminded everyone about cleansing their spirits. About opening up their ears, minds and hearts. So they could listen in a good way, and speak with soft and kind words.

"When you put some medicines in the smudge bowl, like tobacco, you are praying to the Creator," explained Elaine. "The smoke takes the message to the Creator."

Oh, so that's how you pray, River thought.

Elaine continued, "I see we have a couple of new people today. So I'll remind everyone that only one person speaks at a time. That will be the person holding the eagle feather." She brushed the tip of the eagle feather with her aged hands. "What is said in the circle, stays in the circle. You have the right to pass if you are not ready to speak. And Geoff will offer you the smudge if you need it. Maybe we can introduce ourselves again to the group, so the new people can meet us." She passed the feather to Mel on her left.

Mel started. "I'm Mel. Like I said last week, I'm in the middle of dealing with Mom and her mood swings. The other day she sat us all down and told us that she went to the doctor. At first, we were all like 'Oh my god, Mom, don't say cancer.' She started laughing and was like, 'Oh, no. It's just menopause.'"

A few people giggled, including Mel.

"So everyone in the house was relieved that she wasn't going crazy. It's just the next part of her life. We will all try to learn about it. So we can try to make it easier for her by, I don't know, not annoying her and giving her hot flashes."

Elaine nodded with a smile.

"Miigwech," Mel said. She passed the feather to the girl on her left.

"Um, it's my first time here. Oh and I'm Martha by the way. I'm here because I just really need to be around people. I'm feeling kind of lonely, I guess, even though I have a lot of friends, I don't have a lot of family. My mom is never home and I just sit at home alone. So I'm here. I want to learn more about my culture too. Because I just found out I am Métis. My teacher told me about this group a few weeks ago. So thank you for letting me come to this circle."

Elaine smiled at Martha and nodded. Martha passed the feather along to the person on her left.

"Hi," the young man said. His eyes were lowered to his lap, his voice quivering. He was clearly holding onto something painful.

"I'm Dre."

Seconds that felt like minutes absorbed the silence before he spoke again.

"My name is Dre, like I said. Hah . . . And I'm here because, um . . . I moved here from a fly-in, so my mom could go to college. We've been here for six months. And it's just getting harder all the time. I'm missing my home. I miss my family. I miss going for a walk and just bumping into old rez dogs. I miss that. Everyone in the city is in a rush to get somewhere. I don't where they're all going. Geez."

The group giggled.

Dre smirked, then the pain entered his voice again. "I also want to say that my cousin died. That's why I wasn't here last week. The funeral was this past Tuesday. I wasn't even gonna come today. But I thought maybe I needed to talk about it."

Everyone seemed to bow their heads a little when he said this. River wasn't sure why, but she knew there was a reason.

"The hardest part about her passing is that nobody knows why. They say she just mysteriously 'died in her sleep.'" He held his fingers up in the air to make quotation marks. "The autopsy said it was an overdose. But our family is not satisfied with that answer. The police said they couldn't tell if it was an accident, or if someone drugged her. So they have to do a bigger investigation, and we all know how that works in this city." He passed the eagle feather along.

Everyone could see that the next guy was there with Dre. He sat silently, and twirled the eagle feather nervously. He shook his head and passed the feather to River.

"Hi. I'm River." She glanced around and then looked at Dre. "I don't know if this is okay to say right now. But I'm really sorry to hear about your cousin, Dre." The lump in her throat was huge.

Dre nodded at her with his eyes closed.

River went on. "Um, in a new group I'm really shy . . . So yeah . . . um, I'm Ojibwe, and I'm from southern Ontario. And I'm here visiting my dad for the summer. When I go back home my mom and I are moving to the reserve. And, well, I don't know how I feel about that. So that's all I'm going to say for now."

She quickly passed the feather to her left. *These kids have way harder lives than mine*, she thought. *This guy next to me has a dead cousin, and here I am complaining about moving.* River noticed that a couple of people passed. She vowed to give her full attention to every person who spoke in the circle.

"Hey, everyone," said the next girl to speak. "My name is Sage, and I am Cree and Ojibwe. My mom and stepdad are having another baby. That makes four kids in our family now. I wish they would stop having kids. I feel like all I do is take care of the babies while they work. I mean, I like my siblings, but it's a lot. Good birth control for me, I guess."

Smiles and chuckles broke the tension in the room.

"I don't know, I guess I'm also just wanting to spend time with my boyfriend, Tim, without the kids crawling all over us twenty-four-seven."

She smiled at the guy sitting next to her and passed him the feather.

"Hi, I'm Tim. Yup, Sage's boyfriend, Tim. I'm Ojibwe, and I like pizza and fishing."

The group laughed out loud at that.

"Um, I'm just trying to stay positive. And like Sage said, just trying to help out family. I finished high school this year, even though everybody said I wouldn't. I got into the University of Manitoba, and I'm gonna take Economics. Maybe I'll be famous like Wab one day!"

Tim was the only one who giggled at that. But everyone else was still smiling at him.

"Also, I would like to say that I really like coming here every week. Sometimes I talk about hard stuff, and sometimes happy stuff. But even if I don't need to talk, I know that you guys are all here to support me with whatever it is. I hope everyone feels the same. That you feel supported here. Miigwech, Elaine, for joining us and sharing with us. I always look forward to your stories each week."

Tim passed the feather back to Elaine.

"Thank you, everyone, for sharing your hearts and spirits with us today," she said. "Some of you are working through some very hard stuff again this week. I am so sorry to hear about your cousin passing." She nodded at Dre and the guy beside him. "I noticed many of you said a little prayer for her spirit when he spoke of her. I am so happy you remembered that teaching."

Elaine went on, her voice soft, her speaking slow. "This week I want to remind all of you. No matter what you are going through, just like Tim said, you are all here for each other. You could have a fight with your family, or a death, or a hard time at school. Whatever it is. However hard it is. Even if you don't speak directly to each other, you are here to show and to receive support. Our spirits come together, and our ancestors stand behind us as we sit in this circle and talk together."

She sat for a moment, as if she was reflecting.

"I noticed today that some of you were shy to speak, and that's okay. I know we have some new people. Sometimes we share a lot and sometimes we share a little. But I do want you to know that sometimes, the more you share, the better you feel. The second time around the circle, you will have a chance to respond to others if you want, and have a more open dialogue. And then we will do a closing round. We will have a break after the dialogue, and you can have some snacks. I know that's the only reason some of you are here. For the snacks."

The group burst into laughter.

"And just like that, don't forget to laugh, my friends. Don't forget to find the joy in the small moments in life. Let your spirit feel free with laughter."

For the second time, Elaine passed the feather to her left.

July 11

I made it to the youth circle last night. I was so tired, I just couldn't journal when I got home.

I met a few new people. The Elder, Elaine, was amazing. The food was delish. The actual sharing was bittersweet though. We did three rounds of the circle. Some people ended up bawling and sobbing, and I didn't know what to do or to say. Dealing with other people's grief can be super awkward.

Elaine said she would bring us some resources next week on how to deal with our own grief, but also deal with others.' Like what to say and stuff. Elaine reminded us that it's a journey. That we are all on a learning and healing journey in life.

After the circle, I was thinking, I have my mom. I have a really nice home, and farm animals and great friends. I don't have it bad at all. I realized this as I listened to story after story. What feels even worse is that now I feel guilty for feeling like I have any problems at all. I was all, 'Yeah, I'm sad because I have to move. Ohh poor me and my first-world problems.'

But this feeling just doesn't go away. I don't know how to fix this feeling I have. The emptiness. I heard a few other people talk about the same feeling at the circle. It's like a "something's missing" feeling. No one seems to know what it is. I thought Elaine would speak directly to us about how we were feeling exactly. But she just talked about her grandparents when she was small. How they always sang to her in the language, songs about the earth. I didn't really understand what she was trying to say through her stories.

But I felt really lucky to be part of this circle. I think I made a new friend. We are going to see each other at the powwow next month. We added each other on Instagram. I creeped her page. She probably creeped mine. She looks like a cool person.

I think I'll go back to the sharing circle next week. Even though I wonder how anyone could take my problems seriously, I think I might even talk again next week.

CHAPTER 18

I am Sewing One Object to the Other

River and her nokomis sat shoulder to shoulder. Fabric, ribbons, spools of thread and packages of sewing things were scattered on the table. Grace held a ribbon in place with a few straight pins. River held one side of the dress, while her nokomis guided the fabric and ribbon though the sewing machine. They bound them together, one stitch at a time.

River watched her nokomis's hands with awe. They were wrinkled and old. But they held perfect precision while sewing.

"I hope I can sew as good as you one day, Noki." River smiled with her eyes, as she held pins in between her lips.

"You will, my girl," Grace said without looking up. She clipped the final threads from the underside of the dress. "Now that the ribbon is sewn on, the hard part begins. Hand your old granny that box over there." She puckered her lips and turned her head to point with them.

River had never seen anyone in Ontario point with their lips. But she noticed people doing it all the time here. Was it a cultural thing? A Manitoba thing? She picked up a box of round, shiny pieces of tin. They looked like the lids off tuna cans. "These ones, Noki?"

"Yes, those are the ones. First, we have to curl them. These ones here are older ones. You can see they still have the design on the back. We used to make them from tobacco lids when we had nothing else. And these plain silver ones here, with the words *Indian Time* on them. These are the ones your dad and auntie and I made. We sell them on the powwow trail."

Nokomis pulled a silver tool out of the sewing table. It looked like a giant tent peg. "This is what we use to curl or roll the cones. Some people still only curl one cone a night before they go to bed."

"Oh . . . why, Noki?"

"Well the jingle dress is said to be a healing dress. There are a few different versions of this story, but this is the one I know. A long time ago, in the early 1900s, a father had a young daughter who was very ill. He had a vision, or a dream, of a dress he was to make for her. He made her this dress, and as she started to dance and put one foot in front of the other, she started to heal. And this is why they call it the healing dress. The style of dress has changed over the years. They are very fancy nowadays. Even the dance steps have changed."

"But why only one cone a night?"

"Oh, yes, right. I got sidetracked there. Well, some people used to say that you should take your time in your healing journey. They said you should make one cone a night for every day of the year, 365 cones. And some women wear 365 cones on their dresses."

"Whoa, that must be heavy. Will we put 365 on my dress?"

"Well, my girl, culture evolves. And stories evolve. And your noki has always gone against the grain. First of all, if we think of the actual lunar calendar, there's not 365 days in a year, there's 364. The lunar calendar has a full moon every twenty-eight days. And we have our monthly cycle, our moon time, every twenty-eight days too. That's why our monthly cycle as women is called moon time. Then somehow extra days got thrown into some months, and then even a leap year got thrown in there. Not sure what those folks were thinking. Anyway, I believe that even 364 cones are far too heavy to dance in. If you can find some old pictures to look at, before the dance was outlawed, the dresses didn't have a ton of cones on them. They had just enough to make it sound like rain when you danced."

"How do you know all this, Nokomis?"

"Oh, my dear, I just spent a lot of time listening."

"I wish I could live with you, Noki." River thought about what it would be like if she could live with her grandmother, and not worry about anything else. She would love to just sit and listen to stories and drink tea. Her nokomis made the world a better place. River realized that her nokomis grew up in a time when people learned from each other. Now the answer to everything was to Google it. Her nokomis had a ton of knowledge and wisdom, and none of it came from DIY YouTube tutorials.

"You can start by visiting me more, my girl. You are welcome to come and spend whole summers with me again. We can talk over the FaceTime or the Skype too, you know."

River giggled. "Yes, we can, Noki. You're right!" She paused to take in her nokomis's smile. Then she asked another question. "Did you dance when you were small?"

"Well, it was a different time then, my girl. The dancing and ceremonies and any sort of cultural thing had been outlawed for so long. When I was a young girl, powwows were just starting up again. I've told you that there used to be laws in the Indian Act that said we couldn't leave the reserve without a pass. Well, our ceremonies and culture used to be illegal too. I was about twelve when this changed. So when I was about sixteen, just a bit younger than you, my nokomis made me a jingle dress. She remembered how to place the shells on it from when her nokomis taught her. They used shells instead of tin cones back then. Even though it was illegal, our traditions never completely died. We just hid everything from the Indian agents and the churches."

"I can't even imagine, Nokomis."

"Yes, my girl, times have changed so much. So many things have changed in my lifetime, it's unbelievable. And now, I can't keep up fast enough. But a lot of who I am comes from a long time ago. I remember learning how to sew in residential school. It was probably the only good thing that ever came out of that place."

River sat in silence. She thought about all the times she felt empty inside. She wondered why her nokomis never spoke of this emptiness. Surely after everything she had been through, she must have had this empty feeling?

"It's okay, my girl," said her nokomis softly. "We can talk about it another day. We don't want to talk about that stuff while we work on this beautiful dress for you."

River stood abruptly. "Do you want some tea, Nokomis? I feel like some tea."

"Yes, I'd like some tea, River. Just a bit of milk, please." She could hear her nokomis speaking around the lump in her throat.

In the kitchen, River sniffled and used her sleeve to wipe her tears. When she came back to the table, Grace held the dress up in the air. "It looks beautiful, my girl," she said. "We did a great job on the ribbon. We can finish these cones up tonight. Do you like Netflix? We can watch Netflix and roll cones. You have to put the ties through them as well. Then we can sew them onto the dress in the morning, in good light."

River smiled. "Yes, that sounds perfect, Nokomis." She sipped her tea and stared at her healing dress hanging in the window. The silver fabric sparkled in the sun.

July 31

I've been really bad about writing in my journal. So much time has passed already. A lot of things have happened, but each thing just seems to be part of my whole summer. I always thought at home that time passed differently between the school year and the summer. But this is like summer on steroids, with each day flowing into the next like, well, like a river.

There are a few things I want to write down here, so I don't forget. Noki and Dad tell me some pretty important things. I think I should try and remember them.

The stories that Noki tells are about why things are the way they are. And I'm starting to see how her stories of way back are really about the things we are going through now. She told me how her sister lost her status when she married her husband because he was English. But then non-Indigenous women would get a status card just because they married a Native man. She said there have been changes to try to get rid of gender discrimination, and a new generation of people are getting their status back. She talked about not letting people call it a "tax card" at the store. It's a treaty card, a status card, NOT a tax card.

One night, Dad tried to explain treaties to me, and how if you are a Canadian citizen, then you are a treaty person. He says we are all treaty people. Not just Indigenous people, but all people who have to live with the way things were made when treaties were signed. But there were people who didn't sign treaties back in the day. And they don't consider themselves treaty people because they never surrendered lands in the first place! It's so complicated.

I'm surprised how interesting I find this stuff. Dad talked to me about taking Indigenous Studies in the fall. He said I could learn a ton more about the government and how it has treated Indigenous peoples. He even used the word "genocide," which I sort of get.

I've been going to the youth circle every week for the past three weeks, and that's where I've really learned that a person's stories are the way to know them.

Reed, Dre's cousin, finally spoke last week. He said he is sad, but that's not why he hadn't been sharing. He said that he didn't see the point because the police aren't doing their job and finding out what happened to his sister. He is so angry, like he wants to avenge her death or something. But why can't the police keep people safe in the first place? I couldn't help but think about the people dragging the river we drove by when I first got here. Every time I think about it, I just feel sick to my stomach.

A girl named Jenna talked about her boyfriend being messaged by another girl. I mean, I can see how it would make you mad. But then she mentioned that after her mother disappeared last year, everything was just huge and hard to deal with.

A guy named Toby said that he is Cree and something else. But he didn't know what else because he doesn't know who his dad is. He keeps asking his mom, but she won't tell him anything. He said he has tried asking in a kind way, but his mom just makes it into a fight. He said he was really tired because his mother had another party the night before, with tons of people he didn't even know.

"They listen to terrible music and they stink," he said, giggling.

Some of the kids have been talking about reclaiming spaces and places. I don't really understand. But I think it's like being proud of who you are as an Indigenous person, everywhere and anywhere. And making our presence as Indigenous people known, so that we don't stay invisible. One girl she said she is no longer shy to wear her beadwork everywhere, and not just at powwows. She talked about how she used try to blend into the background. She didn't want to bring attention to herself as an Indigenous person in Winnipeg. Now, she says, "No, dammit. This is our land, our space. I'm proud of who I am and who my family is. I am reclaiming this space."

Elaine talked about the different meanings of reclaiming space. Some groups are reclaiming actual lands, and not just public spaces. Lots of new learning for me for sure. All the stories are connected in some way, and all the people are connected by the stories they tell each other. I guess I just have to figure out where my own story fits into all this.

It's pretty ironic that all this learning will stop when and if I go to university.

NAAKWEG

CHAPTER 19
At Noon

Eric drove slowly over the bumps in the field on the west side of the reserve. He parked the car as close to the powwow entrance as he could. River and her nokomis opened their car doors and their feet met the long grass. River cracked open each of the windows as Eric popped the trunk.

River reached into the trunk for her backpack and swung it over her shoulder. She grabbed her feather fan and jingle dress in the same hand. Since Eric was carrying the fold-up chairs and small cooler, River offered to hold her nokomis's hand as they walked toward the white wooden arbour surrounding the dance arena.

Eric placed the three lawn chairs in a row facing the inside of the circle. He set the cooler in between his chair and his mom's, making a little table top. To her right, River noticed a family with a baby. The mom held the baby in her arms, nursing her and staring into her eyes. A cradleboard with a red velvet moss bag and intricate floral pattern beadwork hung from a post on the arbour. River was surprised when an image of her mom flashed through her head.

"I'm going to walk around and look at the craft booths," said River. "Noki, do you want anything?"

"No, I'm okay for now. Thank you, my girl."

"Dad?"

"No, I'm okay too," replied Eric. "Thanks, babe. Come back for Grand Entry. It'll be at high noon."

River smiled at her dad. She tugged at her white mesh trucker hat and pulled her shorts down as she stood. She grabbed her wallet and went to pace slowly in front of the craft vendors.

The vendors made a perfect circle around the dance arena and arbour. The first vendor River came to had classic dream catchers, leather key chains, beaded barrettes and moccasins. River knew that grandmothers always made the most beautiful beaded moccasins. A pair of giant beaded leather gloves with real beaver fur sat on the edge of the table. The Ojibwe floral patterns were vibrant and perfectly stitched. River slid them on and noticed the price of $125. She wished she had that kind of money to spend on mitts. She knew they were worth every penny. She thought that one day, she would make a pair for herself. She yearned to learn how to bead that intricately.

The smell of sweetgrass caught her attention. She saw several braids of sweetgrass on the neighbouring table, along with bundles of wild sage. She could tell the sage was a female plant, a woman's medicine, because of its little purple flowers. She had learned that at the sharing circle the week before. She paid ten dollars for a small bundle of buffalo grass and continued to look at the artistry of the braids before heading to the next booth.

At the side of this booth, a young woman was selling porcupine quill wrapped earrings and regalia sets. River had never seen such beautiful work up close. She fell in love at once with a pair of earrings.

She held them up, looking for a price tag. "How much are these ones?" she asked.

The young woman responded with a smile that spoke of how proud she was of her work. "Those ones are eighty dollars."

River tried to imagine the amount of time that had gone into making a pair of earrings like that. Plucking a porcupine, dyeing and sorting the quills, soaking and wrapping. Then adding beads and the earring wires. She put them down. "They are stunning. Did you make them?"

"Yes, harvested the quills myself," the girl beamed.

"Oh, my goodness, how?"

"Plucked them from roadkill."

"Oh." River was a bit shocked. "Do you have a mirror?"

"Sure, right here." The young woman held up a clunky vanity mirror. She gestured for River to hold the earrings up to her ear. River dangled the two-inch circles from her ears as if she were wearing them. They glistened in the sun.

"They're so sparkly. What's your name, if you don't mind me asking?" River smiled.

"Cedar."

"Oh, what a pretty name."

"What's your name?" Cedar asked.

"River."

"Heck, that's a pretty name too, girl!"

"Thanks! Do you have a business card?"

The young woman laughed. "Heck no! But you can follow me on Instagram. My user name is @cedarsbeadedblingandquills."

"Oh, awesome. Okay, I will for sure. Thanks." River smiled as she walked away, dreaming the earrings were hers.

Then River stopped. Her heel pivoted in the dirt. She walked back to the booth.

"I have to buy these," she said. "They are just absolutely gorgeous."

"Awesome, girl!" said Cedar. "Thanks for the sale! I'm saving to go to college in the fall."

"No, thank *you*, Cedar. Seriously, they are so amazing. These are hard to find where I live. And I'm going to school in the fall too. What are you taking?"

"I'm pre-health. It's a program so I can get into nursing. I want to be a health nurse in my community."

"Wow, that's amazing! Good for you. I have no idea what I want to take yet, so I just started with general arts. But I'm thinking of maybe taking Indigenous Studies."

"So they can tell you how to be an Indian!" Cedar roared with laughter.

River didn't know how to take that joke. But she joined in the laughter and agreed. "*Right?*"

"No, but seriously," said Cedar. "My cousin took a program like that and he really liked it. He ended up in politics."

"Oh, that's cool. Yeah, I really have no idea where I'll end up. Anyways, good luck and thanks again."

"No problem, any time!"

River put on the earrings and walked over to a clearing beneath the maple trees. She crossed her legs as she sat on the grass. There was a slight breeze, so a few wisps of her hair were hanging in her eye. She scrolled through her pictures while fixing her hair, and then took a selfie with her new earrings.

@cedarsbeadedblingandquills #summertime #powwow

It was her first post in weeks.

Right away, @cedarsbeadedblingandquills followed her and commented:

@Riverrunsthroughthefarm thanks for the support girl! They look GORG on you!

From where she was sitting, River could see the Sundance grounds, another white arbour with no roof. She wasn't sure what the Sundance was all about. She pondered, studying the outline of the branches and the colored pieces of cloth flailing in the wind like flags. She stood, dusted off her backside and wandered back toward the family chairs. She noticed familiar faces from afar as she approached the arbour.

"Auntie, it's so good to see you!" River said as she opened her arms wide to hug her aunt Angela. She was visiting from Minnesota with her daughter, Jodi. Both women jumped up to hug River.

"Hol-eee, you're all grown up, cuz!" Jodi whined in her thick Ojibwe accent.

"I know! It's been too long. It's so awesome to see you, Jodi!" River grinned from ear to ear.

"Aren't you dancing today?" Jodi asked.

"Nah, maybe tomorrow. Just not feelin' it yet, even though Noki put so much work into it. I'm too shy." River shrugged her shoulders.

"Yeah, I get it . . . Oh my god, cousin, you *have* to come to the 49 with me tonight. Everybody is going to be there. Let me put my number in your phone, and you can meet me here after dark."

"Ho-kay. But what's a 49?" River asked.

"Ever good, Riv," Jodi laughed.

"No, seriously. What's a 49?"

"Oh, Riv, you've been on the farm for too long. It's like a pow-wow after-party. It's really fun, I promise. Just don't tell your dad you're coming. He probably won't let you go."

River nodded. Would her dad actually stop her from going? After the night at the bar, she didn't think so. "Okay, cool. I'll be there."

Everyone was getting up out of their chairs. The echo of the emcee's voice calling the dancers to the arena rang through the air. As the dancers entered the arena, everyone turned their bodies and bounced up and down. They shifted their weight from one foot to another to the beat of the drum. River felt a shiver in her spine as the vibration of the drum beat in her chest.

She looked at her jingle dress, and wondered what it would be like to be up there dancing. She caught her nokomis's eye. Grace was smiling at her.

MINATAAGWAD NGAMOWIN

CHAPTER 20
The Song Sounds Good

River: Hey Jodi, it's me Riv.

Jodi: Hey CUZZIN!! U coming to the 49?

River: Yeah, I'm just gonna take some stuff back to Dad's. I'll be there. Prolly half an hour.

Jodi: K. Text me when ur close and I'll come and meet u. Tell your dad you're just coming over to visit.

River: Kk.

Warm water soaked the facecloth that River ran over her face and neck. She patted her face dry and applied a little makeup. She put on clean panties and a clean bra instead of taking time for a shower. Her hair got tossed into a messy bun. She tucked her favourite red bandana into her back pocket, in case she got all sweaty again. She brushed her teeth and smiled in the mirror.

She heard her mom's voice. *Clean up after yourself, and don't leave your stuff all over the bathroom sink.* River tidied up the bathroom, leaving it just how she found it. Her mom always made her make the bed when they stayed at other people's houses too. "Leaving a house and not making the bed is poor manners," her mom always said. "And never arrive empty handed."

Her mom's words were always in River's head. They were

starting to haunt her. She knew her mom would be asking 1,492 questions if she could. She would want to know every detail about the powwow, about the 49. River smiled to herself. She loved the fact that there weren't 1,492 questions to answer. And it wasn't like her dad would try to stop her. She texted Jodi.

River: Be there in 10 minutes. I'm walking over.
Jodi: YES!!

River wandered to the back of the powwow grounds. She went past the Sundance area and into the bush. Cedar hedges tickled her bare legs as she trailed behind a line of strangers. It was still black fly season, so the mosquitoes weren't that bad. With one arm raised, shielding her face from branches, River followed the glow of her cell phone as it shone on the pebbled path in front of her. *I wish I had my head lamp*, she thought. The stroll into the bush reminded her of when she was small. She used to spend hours playing behind the barn and in what seemed to be deep forest to her young self. She would spend hours yapping at the farm animals and making tiny villages beneath the willow trees.

The sound of laughter grew closer. A line of strangers before her paraded between two huge boulders that served as the grand threshold to the 49. When she looked up from the path in front of her, she saw women gathered around a circle of men. Each man held a big drum by the loops on its side with one hand, and pounded it in unison with leather-wrapped drumsticks. The women's voices were higher than the men's as they sang a familiar round dance song.

Goosebumps raised under River's long-sleeved shirt, and her heart fluttered. She felt like she was home, even though she was worlds away from where she grew up. Girls barely old enough to be up past eleven held beer cans in the air as they belted out a Nikki Minaj song. Watching them as they sat on the back of the truck tailgate also reminded her of home.

River wandered around the clearing. She noticed that most of the guys were dressed like rappers, some with coloured bandanas. They were spitting lyrics faster than lightning. When River spotted her cousin, Jodi's back was turned to her. River snuck up behind her and poked her in the ribs.

"Hey, cuzzziiiin," River whined in her best rez voice.

Jodi wrapped her arms around her cousin's neck and smooched her on the cheek. "Look at my gorgeous cousin from Ontario, hangin' with the real rez girls now. Breakin' your 49 cherry too. I saw that guy you were looking at today at the powwow. He's over dere." She puckered and pointed with her lips.

As they laughed and took selfies, River pulled the red bandana from her back pocket and poured some water over it. She used it to pat her face, then placed it on her ankle where she had been bitten by a mosquito.

The gang of girls cackled. Normally River was shy, but she wasn't going to waste any time. Jodi would tease her if she didn't drink. And it was only beer, not like the rum she had been drinking at the bar. After she downed two tall boys within half an hour, she felt like she was letting loose. Her legs were numb and wobbly beneath her. She swayed a little, grinning, hoping no one noticed. The girls around her were giggling, and so was she. But she wasn't sure they were all laughing at the same thing.

Suddenly shrill calls interrupted her buzz. Even River knew what that was about. A fight.

"Carmen, no-o-o-o! He's a Northern Rebel!" A girl by the fire was begging her boyfriend to stop fighting.

A sea of ponytails and messy buns swarmed around the brawl. So did cell phone cameras.

"That guy is a Northern Rebel, Jodi?" River slurred.

"Oh my god! Shut up, Riv." Jodi elbowed River in the ribs and whispered in her ear, "Yes, that's a street gang here in Winnipeg. Really scary shit. Don't let anyone hear you talking about them." Jodi shushed her cousin again, and dragged her by the hand toward the crowd. River grabbed her bandana from her ankle so she wouldn't lose it as they rushed into the crowd.

Once she was closer, the sound of the two men grunting and the drunken folk encircling them was strange to River's ears. High school fights didn't sound like this at all.

"He has a knife!"

Everyone in the circle took one step back.

The guy on top, the Northern Rebel, had a knife to Carmen's throat. "If I ever see you in town, you're going to be just another dead Indian," the Northern Rebel snarled, just loud enough for all to hear.

To River's fuzzy brain, it was like being in the middle of a news story. She held up her phone and snapped a photo of the two men on the ground. She posted the picture to Instagram. Then she posted a selfie of herself and Jodi.

The Crazy Crees is a REAL THING YO! #farmgirlinthecity #49 #ontherez

Soon after Carmen stumbled away, the crowd broke up. After a few minutes, everyone seemed to settle down. Things went back to the way they were when River had arrived. Her phone chimed several times, but she ignored it. This was her first 49. She didn't want to have her head in her phone all night.

River spent a few more hours with her cousin and some new

friends, drinking and laughing and dancing. She was surprised at how friendly some people were, and how unfriendly others were. Some glared at her with looks of contempt. She didn't let it bother her too much. She knew she would probably never see any of them again.

CHAPTER 21

I Cover My Head with a Handkerchief

River rolled over to the sound of a barrage of chimes from her cell phone. It was not how she wanted to wake up the morning after the 49. She barely opened her eyes to read the messages. She reached for her water bottle. Her mouth was dry, her breath wretched. Her head was pounding.

It wasn't clear who was messaging her, who was commenting on her Instagram photos. She was stunned to find more than a hundred comments on one of her pictures. Her number of followers had gone from 67 to 367 overnight.

WTF? she thought.

She opened the photos — mostly selfies of her and her cousin and her friends from the 49. She swiped through and saw the picture of the two men fighting. She couldn't remember posting it, but there it was. Her sense of urgency to read the comments grew as she scanned them. The whole time she wondered why she would post something like that on Instagram. Her judgement must have been skewed by the many tall boys she drank. Her forehead wrinkled as she started to read.

@SSCXO: @Riverrunsthroughthefarm You better step off B*TCH!

@Rezsister: @Riverrunsthroughthefarm WTF FARM GIRL. You're so dead.

@49lover: @Riverrunsthroughthefarm You have no idea what you have gotten yourself into squaw. Watch your back.

She sat up straight in her bed.

Oh my god, what have I done?

She leaped out of bed and ran to the front door, her socks sliding down each stair. She went outside to make sure she had perfect cell phone reception. She texted her cousin.

River: JODI. WHAT HAVE I DONE?

Jodi: What do u mean?

River: Check my Instagram

Jodi: Oh shit.

River: What?!

Jodi: You pissed off one of "the girls" from the Northern Rebels. Why in the hell did you post that picture? I told you to not even talk about them, never mind post a damn picture! And you have a damn red bandana in your hand! OMG I didn't even see that! OMG, you are gonna eat so much shit from this.

River: WHAT!? WHY! I had a mosquito bite! What is happening? What kind of shit? By those pictures? I didn't even realize I posted them!

Jodi: Yeah, um, you should probably take them down.

River: YES. Ok I'll do it now.

Jodi: K let me know what happens.

River: Kk.

River scrolled through and deleted all of the photos from the 49. She hoped that this would be the end of it. The end of the comments and threats. She decided that posting some kind of response would be a good idea to clear the air.

@Riverrunsthroughthefarm: Please forgive me for my mistake. Photos have been removed.

River headed into the kitchen to find her dad.

"Dad," her voice cracked.

"What is it, Riv?" Her dad looked up with his eyes wide.

"I think I made a big mistake last night."

"Why . . . what? Tell me."

"Well, me and Jodi ended up at the 49." *Not technically a lie*, she thought. "I think I had too many beers. And Jodi and her friends and I were taking selfies. And then there was a fight, and I guess I took some pictures," she rambled. "I posted them on Instagram. I didn't realize what I was doing at the time. And I woke up to like a million new followers and hate messages. I don't know what to do, Dad."

"Geez, eh."

"Dad. What do I do?"

"Well, did you take them down?"

"Yes. And I posted an apology as well."

"Let me see the pictures you posted."

River scrolled through her photos and showed him one at a time.

"Well, first of all, you posted the actual fight. Geez. That's terrible."

"DAD!"

"No, I mean it's terrible the way kids are carrying on all violent and stuff."

He continued to scroll. "There, that one, look at this picture. You're taking a selfie with these guys in behind. You have that red bandana in your hand, and they have on white bandanas."

"Bandanas? What do bandanas have to do with anything? I had a mosquito bite, and I was hot. I poured water on it. It's just a BANDANA. It doesn't mean anything."

"Well, it does to them," her dad sighed. "Different coloured bandanas are a gang thing."

"And you didn't think to tell me this? Now what do I do, Dad? I apologized, but like, now what? Is everything just fine now? Like, I don't have to worry?"

"I don't know, dear. What are they going to do about it? Sit behind their keyboards firing threats at you? Big deal. Change your account or something."

"Gosh, what a mess. I don't think it's that simple. I didn't mean for any of this to happen, Dad." River could see the sympathy in her dad's eyes for her innocence. But that didn't help her now. "I think I'll just lie low for a bit on social media. I can't read all those nasty comments. These people don't even know me, and they are saying all kinds of mean things. There are even threats."

"River, it's a different life out here," said Eric. "The communities here are not like the ones in southern Ontario. It's like where you live is in this bubble, different from the rest of the country."

"What are you talking about, Dad?"

"I think you are really lucky that you have been protected from all of this. But that can get you into trouble. What you did — posting pictures of you with a red bandana in front of people fighting wearing white bandanas — upset people. Maybe they thought it was some kind of turf thing. Remember, Riv, they don't know who you are. They don't know that farm girls from southern Ontario have no idea what bandanas represent here in this city. They have no idea that this is a foreign world to you."

"Well, now what?"

"I guess just wait it out and see, babe."

"Okay."

Grace was listening to the exchange between her son and granddaughter. She piped up from the living room, "River, come here for a sec, my girl."

River walked into the living room. She curled up on the couch beside her grandmother, holding her arm and resting her head on her shoulder. Her nokomis smelled like Lily of the Valley perfume.

Grace rested her wrinkled hand on River's. "River, don't let them bother you on the inter-web like that. Just stay off of there for a while. Maybe spend some more time with your granny. Maybe spend some more time at the powwow in your healing dress, or maybe with Mother Earth. She's a healer, you know. You can send her your feelings."

"You know, Noki," River said, "that sounds like exactly what I need right about now."

"Wanna head over to the powwow, my girl?"

"Yes, I do. But somehow, I don't think that's the best idea for today, Nokomis."

Her grandmother nodded. "What if we spend the day in the garden? You can give all that pain back to the earth."

River had no idea what her nokomis meant by that. But she patted her hand. "That is an excellent idea, Nokomis."

River started upstairs. But then she turned and came down again. "I only have this crappy elastic that doesn't stretch anymore. Or this red bandana, which I'll never ever wear around here again. Do you have anything I can use for my hair, Noki?"

"I have just the thing, my girl." Grace stood up and climbed the stairs.

"I had to look in a box under my bed," Grace said as she returned down the stairs. "This is something your old granny made a long, long time ago. I made it when my hands still worked really well and I could do a lot of beading. I was on a plane going to Germany with your dad, and we ended up meeting this old Crow man. He taught me how to use these tiny beads. They're size fifteen, called Charlottes."

Grace placed the beaded barrette in River's hands and covered them with hers. "This is yours now, River. When you're a nokomis, you can give it to your granddaughter. You might want to give it your daughter. But if you can wait, there's something special about gifting it to your granddaughter. You have a different kind of love for your grandchildren. You'll see."

River felt her eyes welling up at her nokomis's soft words. She looked down and saw the beautiful contrasting colors. She could see that the Ojibwe floral patterns were old, from way back in the day. River thought it made the barrette even more special.

"Miigwech, Nokomis." River smiled and squeezed her nokomis tight.

August 8

What have I done?! I don't know. And I can't even guess at what it means. I don't think anyone is hurt by this, right? I think I just made a ton of people upset. I can't believe the pics would spread that fast.

Dad might be right. I guess I am sheltered and naive. Is life here always this dangerous? Does every single teenager live like this? It can't be true. It just can't be. Maybe I'll find out more when I go to the sharing circle on Saturday. I hope they will listen. I hope they can help me.

Why didn't Dad say anything about how dangerous it was until it was too late? He was fine with letting me go off with Russell. At that party I saw guys wearing red bandanas. They must have been gang members. It's all very well to call me naive now, but why didn't Dad try to keep me out of trouble? And I have the feeling that his idea of waiting this out might not be the best way to deal with it.

For the first time since I got here, I feel like I really need my mom. Dad and Noki are awesome, but I'm starting to feel really sad and really scared. So much has happened in the last six weeks. Things have been going so fast. I feel kind of lost, and that I'm missing things. I'm mad at myself for not dancing at the powwow. Who cares if I can't stop on the beat. Maybe if I had danced that day, I wouldn't be in this mess.

Why did I drink? That's what Mom would ask me if she were here.

I would say I drank because I was so uptight and tense and stressed. If I think about it, I see it's probably because I'm trying to be something or someone I'm not. I don't know if it's me trying to be more Native. Or less Native, if that makes any sense. Like how can you be more or less Native than you are?

Sometimes I wonder what my friends are doing. I bet their summer isn't anything like mine! I wonder if they miss me. Sometimes I miss them. But then it's like they're not part of my life at all anymore. It's really weird how actual distance can make you feel more distant from your old life, or old self or old friends. We've texted some back and forth. But it's not the same as it used to be. I'm not sure how I feel about it.

It's only when I'm with Nokomis that anything makes any sense. We're going to spend the rest of the week in the garden. She keeps saying I can send my feelings to the earth, whatever that means. I feel like half the time I don't get what she is trying to tell me with her stories and her talk about Mother Earth. It's like she speaks in code or something. Anyway. We are going to pick the beans, and pickle some beets this week.

We're having burgers tonight for dinner. I better get my butt in gear. There's lots of work to be done. At least I feel at home in the garden. Reminds me of the farm.

CHAPTER 22

The Girls Hurt the Child

River could feel the gravel beneath her feet poke through the thin soles of her moccasins. Just a quick run to the store on the rez, but she still needed a shirt and shoes to be served. She grabbed some hamburger buns from the slightly rusty silver bread rack. Then she made her way through the narrow aisles cluttered with non-perishables and travel-size convenience items.

She grabbed some gum at the counter and tapped her debit card against the machine. As she left the store, she unwrapped a piece of gum and shoved the tiny silver wrapper in the little pocket in her jean shorts. Her red bandana peered from her pocket. *Geez, I thought I left this at home*, she thought.

"Hey, farm girl!"

River looked up. There were two girls sitting on the ice box beside the store. It was the taller girl with broad shoulders who was calling to her.

"You're not from around here, are you?" the girl asked.

River shook her head no. She was still standing with the hamburger buns in both hands.

"Who do you think you are, posting pictures like that on the internet?" asked the other girl. She was shorter and heavier, and had a blonde streak in her long black bangs. She had resting grouchy face, which made the hair on River's arms stand up.

"You got a problem with us?" the blonde-streak girl yelled. She spat on the ground near River's feet.

"No . . . I . . . I'm sorry. I had no idea what I was doing." River's voice was hoarse.

"We don't like girls like you coming into our rez. Do we, Brianna?" The broad-shouldered girl checked with the girl beside her. "You think you can pretend you're one of us? When you are *not*."

"Look at how white her skin is, Steph," said the other girl, then turned back on River. "Bitch, you're whiter than a damn Métis. You're not one of us, you didn't grow up here. You don't know our struggles. How dare you pretend you are like us. Probably just use your status card to get out of tax and for a free education."

"What the hell are you talking about?" River blurted.

"You got something to say to us, white girl? You damn apple. Red on the outside, white on the inside!" Steph taunted.

"What? No! What's happening here?" River took one step back as the two girls stood up and approached her.

"This is what's happening, bitch!" Brianna ploughed toward River and swung with her fist, which met with River's jaw.

Blood smeared the side of Eric's car window. River had never been punched in the face before. She grabbed her jaw and bent over in pain, dropping the hamburger buns on the gravel.

Steph's boot struck the back of River's knee. River fell to the ground, screaming in pain. Both girls stomped on River's foot and calf. All River could do was curl into the fetal position beside her dad's car. She wept. *What is happening? Why is this happening? What is happening?* The thoughts raced on a loop through River's mind.

"Take a selfie now, bitch, for all your little white farm friends to see," River heard. Then the girls stood back and walked away.

A woman came out of the store and ran over to River's side.

"Oh my god! Are you okay, hon?" the woman asked. "What the hell is wrong with you two?" she screamed at the girls, who were now running.

River winced and sat up. "Yeah, it's nothing, I'm okay. I just want to go home." She dug for her keys, but instead found the red bandana. She carefully wiped the blood from the car window. She fiddled for the keys in her pocket as she got in. Her hands shook as she started the car and pulled away from the store.

"UGHH!" River screamed as she drove away. She slammed the palm of her hand against the steering wheel. *What have I done, what have I done, what have I done?*

Knowing she needed to calm down, she pulled over to compose herself. She got out her cell phone and noticed there were several new notifications.

Someone had taken a snapshot of her profile picture. It showed her wearing a red bandana.

So this is the bitch who originally posted the fight at the 49. A damn apple. She's not even from our rez! She's an apple from the Wanabe Tribe.
@Riverrunsthroughthefarm
#lookatthisbitch #deadfarmgirl #justdoitalready

Her name was tagged and the threats in the comment threads were growing by the minute.

AnneKOIxo_: @Riverrunsthroughthefarm Go back to where you came from you dumb bitch!
GINA99: @Riverrunsthroughthefarm You're f**king dead you wannabe.
AllinaLove: @Riverrunsthroughthefarm You are gonna wish you killed yourself, after you find out what they are going to do to you

Sassy_jules_rules_da_rez: @Riverrunsthroughthefarm What you got today was just the beginning, watch your f**king back white girl

Mia.is.da.bomb: @Riverrunsthroughthefarm This is our turf SLUT. We saw you sleeping with Russell in the North End. Stay away from our boyz!

River's hand shook as she scrolled through. Her heart was pounding, and her leg started to shake her foot on the brake. She threw her phone on the passenger seat and sped back to the house.

As she pulled up the driveway, Eric came out to meet her. "What the hell happened to you, River?" he asked when he saw her face.

"Oh, nothing, Dad." Her chuckle sounded fake, even to her. She babbled as she followed her dad into the house. "I am so clumsy sometimes. I tripped and fell. I hit my chin against the car. I didn't put my hands out because I didn't want to squish the hamburger buns. I feel so stupid . . . I was wearing my mocs and I just tripped I guess."

"Oh . . ." Eric sighed. He raised one eyebrow. "You know, I'm not convinced."

River mustered another fake laugh. "Dad, really. I can't believe I just fell like that!"

Eric didn't take his eyes off River as he set the table. "So did you cry?"

"No, I'm a farm girl, Dad. I can handle a little tumble in the dirt."

"Then why is there mascara running down your cheek?"

River hung her head. "Dad, don't worry. It's nothing. I'm fine."

"River, word travels on the rez. It's like there's instant smoke signals or something. And the moccasin telegraph doesn't take long, you know. Either *you* tell me . . . or I'll find out the gossip from my neighbour Penny, in like, a minute."

Tears streamed down River's cheeks. But she didn't make a peep. "Dad, can I just skip dinner tonight?" she pleaded. "Can I just rest for a bit? And then I'll tell you everything."

"Okay, but I need to know if you are okay first. And who did this to you."

"Dad, just let me clean up first."

"Okay. Well, let me get you a cloth at least."

"Where's Nokomis?"

"She's at bingo."

"Oh, good. I don't want her to know."

"Know what?"

"Dad!"

"Okay, okay. Go rest for a bit. But when I come up, I'll be expecting an explanation."

"Okay."

"Pinky swear?" Eric held out the smallest finger of his right hand.

River latched hers to his. "Pinky swear, Dad."

August 9

So that happened. I totally got hazed yesterday.

First of all, I'm not a slut. I didn't sleep with anyone. Second of all, I took the pictures down as soon as I realized they upset people. Third of all, I never once pretended to be anything I wasn't. I wear a damn red bandana because it's hot outside and to keep my hair out of my face. No other reason.

I'm starting to get why Mom never wanted me to grow up here. She was trying to protect me. But I bet people wouldn't target me with distrust if I grew up here on the rez. I'm not an apple. I'm not white on the inside, and red on the outside. But that doesn't make sense with them calling me white, does it? So I'm too brown for a small town and not brown enough for the rez.

I'm getting my face kicked in and all I could think about is Nokomis and Elaine. I could almost see them standing around me. But what were they trying to tell me?

NGII-WIISGENDIMO'AA

CHAPTER 23
I Hurt His Feelings

River's nokomis knocked softly on the bedroom door. "River, can I come in?"

River opened the door. Eric was right behind his mother.

"Dad?" River glared. "You told."

"What?" asked Eric, holding up his hands. "She needs to know. She's smarter than me at this stuff."

"River, what happened?" asked her nokomis. "Who did this to you? Was it two teenage girls at the store?"

"How do you know that, Noki?"

"Word travels fast at bingo. All the grannies have cell phones too, you know."

"Oh my god. Yes. I got jumped at the store by these two girls. They were saying I was, like, white, and I don't belong here. That kinda stuff."

"Gee whiz, River," said her nokomis. "Ever sad, those girls. I don't know why they act like that. I think I know them. They have done that before, and they never seem to get caught. No one ever calls them out on their actions."

"Why?"

"They might be gang affiliated," suggested Eric. "And no one wants to mess with that. So they just lie low until it smooths over, or is forgotten. Or they move on to the next person."

"So this is normal? This would never happen where I live." River stood lifeless with her hands by her side.

Eric hung his head and looked at his mother.

Her nokomis shook her head in disbelief. "I'll arrange for a healing and justice circle. River, we will work through this together. Don't you worry, my girl. Your old noki knows exactly what to do."

River looked back at her dad. He just shrugged and mouthed, "I told you so."

* * *

River answered her phone.

"Hi, Josh."

"Umm . . . are you okay? What's going on?"

"Why? What do you mean?"

"I just saw that nasty post you were tagged in."

"I don't know what's going on. I honestly don't know what to say to you, Josh."

"Well, are you gonna tell me what happened? We haven't talked in more than a month. This isn't like us at all. It's not like you at all. It's like I don't even know you anymore."

"Okay. Well. I got hazed at the store today. Some crazy rez girls, who were clearly mistaken about my intentions, just called me out. They beat me up and then posted some lies online about me. I just told Dad and Nokomis what happened to me. Noki is calling for a healing-justice circle thing. She says she knows the girls and they have done this before."

"And?" Josh demanded.

River paused. "And what?"

"I know this might be bad timing. But can you at least tell me what it meant in the comments when it said 'we saw you sleeping with Russell in the North End'?"

"Um . . . yeah . . . I don't know. It's kind of a long story. And it isn't what it seems like, I swear."

"Hmmm. Okay."

The silence grew.

"I'm listening," said Josh with an edge in his voice.

"Well . . . I was going to wait and tell you in person when I got back. I honestly haven't even thought about it really. I went to a party and got wasted. I ended up sleeping in the same bed as this guy, because it was a really scary place in the North End, and I didn't feel safe. But nothing happened, I SWEAR."

"Nice." The hurt in Josh's voice pierced River's ears.

"Josh."

"So . . . um . . . I'm just supposed to believe you? Believe that nothing happened?"

"Why would I lie to you, Josh?"

"I don't know, River. It all seems pretty dramatic. And even if you didn't have sex with the guy, it's not like you're having sex with me. I've been patient, River, but now it looks like 'nothing' is what's been happening between you and me all these years. You haven't told me anything that has been going on since you left. Talk to me, River."

River felt she couldn't even start explaining to Josh. "Josh, I can't. Maybe we need a break."

"What are you saying? I'm calling to see if you're *okay*. Calling to see if this is *true*. You say it *sort of is*. And now you are telling me we need *a break*? What is happening with you, River?"

"Josh, all I know is that I seriously need to figure some stuff out. It's more complicated than it seems. I have no idea how I got into this one. Or how to dig myself out. I really don't want to drag you into all of this."

"But you already have, River. This sounds like a lot of 'It's not you, it's me.' And I'm not buying it."

"Can I call you in like a week and we can talk more, when I get some stuff figured out?"

"Don't bother," Josh snapped as he hung up the phone.

CHAPTER 24

It Causes or Brings Shame

The circle was small, only eleven chairs. River sat in one and looked at the opening in the eastern doorway. By now she knew that the eastern door was always left open to invite the ancestors in.

When she saw who entered after her, her jaw hit the floor. Her heart pounded in her chest. It was Russell. He sat down to her left. He shuffled his bag and then his sparkling eyes met hers.

"Hi, River." Russell's voice was soft.

"Um, hey?" she whispered, confused.

"How are you?" he asked.

"I'm okay . . . and you?" Her eyes darted around the room, looking for clues as to why Russell was there.

"Did you miss me?" He winked. He moved closer beside her.

"What are you doing here?" she finally asked. Even though she wasn't sure she wanted the answer.

"I'm a community youth outreach worker."

It took a minute for his words to sink in. Was she some kind of social experiment for him? Was that why she hadn't heard back from him since that night? "And do you reach out and sleep with all the youth you work with?" she hissed. Still stinging from talking to Josh, the anger River felt found a good target in Russell.

"River, it wasn't like that at all. And we didn't sleep together," he responded quietly.

She was trying to keep her tone cool and her volume low. "Okay, do you sleep BESIDE . . ."

She was distracted by the opening of the main door. In walked the two young girls from the store and a young man probably her age. Behind them were a man and a woman who looked to be their parents, and a police officer in uniform. They all sat down in the circle. Right after them, River's dad and nokomis sat down in the circle as well.

The circle began. River had been told that the young woman who was running the healing circle was named Jennifer. She wore beaded earrings, jeans and a fitted black T-shirt. River thought Jennifer was the perfect amount of chubby in all the right places. Her cheekbones were high and her skin was radiant. But what was most obvious was the kindness and peace that seemed to flow off her. River could not stop staring at her glow.

They all stood, and started the circle with a smudge. The smell of the burning sage grounded River like nothing else. She smudged her eyes, her ears, her heart and her body, to clear her mind and listen with an open heart. She pleaded with her inner self to let go of all thoughts of Russell, all thoughts of Josh. It wasn't about them. This was about her. She spoke to the Creator and asked that the Great Spirit help her on this journey. She asked the Creator for a sign or something that would show her the path she was supposed to be on. She was tired of feeling lost. She was tired of feeling like she had no real home of her own. She had a hard time feeling like she belonged anywhere. The only place she felt she belonged was in the presence of the smudge. She stood with a lump in her throat, waiting for the others to finish.

Jennifer sat in the first chair to the left of the eastern doorway. She swung her hair behind her back with her left hand and tucked the other side behind her ear.

"Miigwech, Nanaboozhoo," Jennifer began, "Waussi-noodae Kwe Ninidishniikaaz, Maang dodem, Long Plains ndoongabaa. Thank you, everyone, for joining us. I just thanked the Creator for joining us, and I introduced myself to the Creator in my spirit name. My name is Northern Lights Woman. I'm from the loon clan, and I am from Long Plains First Nation. I want to start by acknowledging the Treaty One territory that we are gathered on here today. It's important we remember our ancestors, the ones who came before us, as we work here today, for the ones who will come after us."

She looked around the room and made eye contact with almost everyone as she spoke.

"I also want to thank everyone for having the courage to show up for today's circle. This is not an easy circle to join, a circle to find the truth, to find justice. The work we do here today will be hard. But the Creator doesn't put lessons in our way that we can't handle."

She shifted her weight in her chair. "We will start by going around the circle and introducing ourselves. Much like a sharing circle, when we pass the feather around, please respect the person who is speaking by listening carefully and not interrupting. You do have the right to pass if you're not ready to speak. But since this is a restorative circle, you will be asked to participate at some point. If you need the smudge, please help yourself. We have people here to support you if you need a break. There is also water underneath your chair."

She held the eagle feather with turquoise peyote stitching on the shaft. Then she passed it to the boy who was sitting on her left.

He cleared his throat, then spoke. "My name is Gerald, and I am from the rez here. I'm here to support my two sisters, Stephanie and Brianna. They are the abusers, I guess." He passed the feather to the woman on his left.

"My name is Michelle, and I am Brianna and Stephanie's mother." River could see she was upset. Her knee was shaking. She passed the feather to the man on her left.

"My name is Kyle. I am the father of Brianna and Stephanie, and our son Gerald." He passed the feather to one of his daughters and sat stiffly, with his arms crossed against his chest.

"My name is Brianna," the girl with the blonde streak in her hair said. She threw the feather into her sister's hands beside her.

"My name is Stephanie," the taller girl said. River could tell from their body language that she was the follower and her sister was the ringleader. Stephanie passed the feather to the man in uniform.

"I'm Sergeant Michael Johnston. I am here from the Anishnaabek Police Service." He passed the feather to his left.

"Boozhoo," River's nokomis began. "Gchi Nodin Kwe Nidiishnaakaz, Waawaashkeshi dodem. I am from the community here as well, and I am Grace, the grandmother of River." She passed the feather to her son.

"Hello, everyone. My name is Eric. I am River's dad." He passed the feather to his daughter.

"Uh," River's voice cracked. The two girls squirmed in their chairs. "My name is River. And I believe you are all here because of me." River felt goosebumps on her arms. She passed the feather to her left. Russell looked deep into River's eyes as he received the feather from her.

"Boozhoo," Russell began. "Biidaaban Ndishniikaaz, Maayungm dodem, Pukatawagan Dongaabaa. My English name is Russell. My spirit name means the First Light in the Morning. I'm wolf clan from Puk, and I am the youth outreach worker for Winnipeg Anishnaabek Health Services. I'm here today to offer support to young people on both sides of this conflict."

He leaned across the eastern door and passed the feather back to Jennifer, who began the second round of the healing circle.

She said, "This time as we take turns speaking, I'd like you to focus on why you are here and speak of anything you need resolved. Speak your needs and your reflections. Be mindful that this round can be very difficult. Truths that people are not ready to hear might be told. Remember that you need to be respectful, to not interrupt anyone and wait your turn to speak." She passed the feather to Gerald.

"I don't think I should start. All I know is that this girl, River, posted some pictures that probably got her into trouble. My sisters beat her up, and now we're here." He slouched in his chair as he passed the feather to his mother.

Michelle was already sobbing. "The police showed up at my door two nights ago, telling me that my two girls had been involved in an assault. Of course, the first thing I thought was that they were the victims. Never in a million years did I ever think I would be sitting here with my two girls facing charges for assault."

Her knee bounced, and her hands twirled the feather as she spoke. "You know, I'm so disappointed that my girls were involved in something like this." She started crying again. Jennifer handed her a bunch of tissues. "My two baby girls, who I tried to raise right. Who come from a good family, who have never been in trouble. Who do well in school, who seem to be these kind, normal girls . . ." She shook her head and looked at her daughters. "I can't believe you two attacked this girl at the store. What were you thinking? Why would you do something like this? Tell us all why you did this."

As she passed the feather to her husband, her hands were shaking. River thought about her mom. How would her mom feel if River did what this woman's daughters had done? River didn't think she would ever attack someone out of hate. But she had done some things she wasn't proud of since she left home.

Kyle took the feather and a deep breath. He leaned forward with his elbows on his knees and spoke directly to his daughters with the feather in his hands. "You know, I always thought it was going to be Gerald who would bring the police to the house. And here it is my two beautiful daughters. Do you know that when you were born, Brianna, I never took another drink after that? Your mother and I have done everything in our power to raise you right. To give you a good home, a loving home. To make sure you had the things you needed. I would expect this from kids who come from troubled homes. But, holy cow, we have a good life, girls." His voice cracked a little. "I just want to know why I guess. What on earth possessed you to hurt another young woman. Another young Indigenous woman who is supposed to be your sister. You are supposed to raise each other up, not bring each other down. We still love you. I still love you. But I am heartbroken. I am truly heartbroken."

He wiped the tears from his eyes with tissues that his wife slipped to him. He passed the feather to his daughter Stephanie.

This is it, thought River. *Finally I'll know why this happened.*

MIISH MIGIZI MIIGWAN

CHAPTER 25

Pass the Eagle Feather

Stephanie sat holding the feather, sobbing. "I want to talk, I just can't yet," she said.

"Whenever you're ready, Steph," Jennifer reassured her.

The room was silent. River remembered her nokomis talking about how silence has come to make people feel uncomfortable. But in the old ways, silence was not a negative thing.

Finally, Stephanie began through the streams of her tears. "I don't know why I followed along this whole time. It's not like I ever imagined myself doing this stuff or being a part of it. When we went to the 49, there was this girl recruiting members for a new girl gang they were trying to start. They told us all we had to do was beat up the farm girl and we would be in. We asked around and we knew she was just here for the summer. So we thought this would all just go away really quick and be over. It seemed too easy." She turned to her father. "Dad, don't you see? We need protection now if we want to hang out in the city. With all the damn girls that end up floating in the Red River, how are we supposed to stay safe? You need a city family to keep you safe from perverts and Indian killers." She paused again.

"I guess I'm sorry. I never thought it would end up like this. After talking to the police, I realized that I don't want to have anything to do with gang life." She wiped her nose and passed the feather to her sister.

Brianna was stoic. Cold. "What can I say? We need protection. A gang can keep us safe. It's not such a big thing — a punch and a couple of kicks. We knew she was leaving at the end of summer anyways, so we wouldn't have to see her. I don't have anything against this girl. But I'll do what I have to to keep my sister and me safe." She passed the feather to the police sergeant.

River felt like her head might explode. The only way these girls could feel safe was by hurting her. The idea shook her to the core. Before this summer, she had never thought that just being who she was would put her in danger. Or that it would be up to the people around her to try to protect her or get justice if something did happen to her.

For a policeman, Sergeant Johnston spoke very softly. "You know, I have two girls your age . . . and this whole situation really hit home for me. I know exactly what these young women are talking about when they say they are scared to be in the city alone. I've been there when a young woman was pulled from the river. I'd never wish that on my worst enemy. And I never want to be the officer that has to tell a mom her daughter was found dead in a garbage bag. Yet that is my job. I sit here with a lump in my throat today, because I know in my heart that nobody wants to be here, and nobody wants to be in this situation."

He paused. He sat up straight and took a deep breath. "I agreed to this circle because I have known both families for a very long time. I know that Kyle's girls were good kids when they were small. I know that Eric's girl is not from here. She's from a completely different world, and possibly had no idea what she was walking into. You know, this circle, it doesn't make everything go away. And doesn't fix anything in the bigger picture. I think that if Stephanie and Brianna continue to make decisions like this after we leave here, they will be certainly seeing the inside of a cell in the future. Girls, this might be your one and only chance. And I hope you realize this chance that you have been given. Because many people are not afforded the chance to make things right in their lives. River and her family have not decided yet if they want to press charges. And after this circle, it might not be up to them. That's all I have to say. Miigwech." He passed the feather to River's nokomis.

"Thank you, Michael. I have known you and your family since you were small. I know you come from a good family. I am thankful you agreed to this circle here today. I, too, don't want to see anything terrible happen to these girls. Any of them. I do think that if it were young men involved, we would be having a very different conversation. We would probably be saying things like *I always knew this would happen.* We heard that about Gerald. Gerald's parents are waiting for him to do something to screw up."

Gerald was nodding his head in agreement.

"I have also known this family for a very long time. I have watched these young girls grow up in the community. I know that Michelle and Kyle have worked hard to overcome all the challenges life has thrown at them. And when I think of my River, I know she is struggling to find her place, to find herself. I hate to think that this has set her back. For a young woman like my granddaughter to experience this. She should have been welcomed in, welcomed home, by the youth in our community. It really makes me sad. It makes me feel like we as Elders haven't done our job."

She took a sip of water.

"This situation reminds me of a growing tree. On one side of the tree there is moss growing. On the other side of the tree, the leaves get more water, so the leaves are greener. It's the same tree. It lives in the same earth. It has the same roots. But if you stand on one side of the tree, you see something very different than the other side. I think that the thing to remember is that the roots are what's important. Without healthy roots, the tree does not grow. And that is all I have to say."

River's heart sank. The lump in her throat bulged. Another one of her nokomis's mystifying stories. But this time she let the words sink into what she was feeling. For the first time, she felt she almost got it.

Eric accepted the feather from his mother. "I always find it hard to follow a wise Elder in circle," he quipped. The adults chuckled.

"I think Mom is right. And Sergeant Johnston is right. This is out of character for all of the girls. I am really happy that we were all able to come here today, to meet in this way. I don't know you two girls very well at all. But I do know your parents are good people. I also know that my daughter doesn't deserve any of this. I can't speak for her, but I do know that much of this is because of her sheltered upbringing. She has no idea what it's like in this part of the country. She doesn't even drink. And here I am taking her to a bar for the first time, thinking that this will make me a cool dad. I think I am trying to make up for all the times I haven't been there for her in her life. I haven't had to protect her growing up. I haven't set any limits for her while she's been here. What I do see is her internal struggle. River, I can't imagine what this has done to your spirit. You had to experience the dark side of the city way too fast, and too soon. And for that, and for these things I spoke of, I am truly sorry, my girl." He handed the feather to River.

River's hand shook. She was stunned by her dad's confessions. She didn't know how to address them. So she started with what was around her. "I first have to say, I have never been in a healing and justice circle before. This is completely new to me. Actually, there are a lot of things that are new to me here. When I first got here, I

145

thought I knew exactly what I was going to say. I came here feeling very defensive. I came here ready to accuse. And as I sit here and listen to all of you speak, I realize my mind has changed."

River took a deep breath. She thought of what her nokomis said about the tree. "I ended up at my dad's this summer because I was running away from stuff that was going on at home. And since getting here, I found out that when I have a few drinks, I am not in complete control of what I am doing or saying. I shouldn't have posted those things from the 49. I should have tried harder to understand how things are here. I take responsibility for coming here to Winnipeg and assuming that I understood how things work. How people feel. I don't want to be someone who just comes here and messes things up. And then goes back to my sheltered little life. This whole thing has made me think about who I am as a person. And who I don't want to be."

River looked at Russell. His eyes met hers with kindness. She passed the feather to him.

"I'll keep this short," said Russell. "It sounds like you all have done a lot of the hard reflecting before you even got here. Usually I have much more work to do in these circles. But if any of you kids want to talk more, you know how to reach me. Stephanie, Brianna, we can talk about ways to feel safer without gang involvement. Or how to try to get the gangs to leave you and other people alone. Like Elder Grace said, all of you have had a look at a different side of the tree. I am so thankful that all of you have participated with honesty and integrity here today. Your words are truly appreciated. Miigwech."

Brianna and Stephanie's mother sniffled a bit more as Russell passed the feather to Jennifer.

"Okay, girls, so if you are ready we can head to the back yard, for the second part of our healing journey, the sweat."

CHAPTER 26
The Cedar Lodge

Russell leaned over to River and stuck out his hand for her to shake.

River had been surprised to see how supportive Russell was. How wise he was to bring them all back to the Elder's words. To her nokomis's words. She liked this side of Russell. He seemed like a different guy from the one she had left the bar with. For the first time, it struck her that going to the party might be part of his job. That knowing gang members and kids in trouble was one way he could be there to help. He didn't know how young and naive River was when they met. But he stayed with her and did his best to make her feel safe.

"Oh, come on, give me a hug," River said with a smile.

"Good luck on your journey, River," he said as they hugged.

"Thank you, Russell. You too."

Jennifer walked the girls to the back yard of the centre. "I didn't want to ask you all in front of everyone. But are any of you girls on your moon time?"

The other girls shook their heads no.

River's eyes were wide. "No, I'm not. Why?"

"Nothing, really. It's just that normally women don't go into ceremony with others when they are on their moon time. But we're all good!"

"Oh. Okay. Uh, can I ask why? Sorry, I don't know anything about this."

"No problem, River," replied Jennifer. "It's a woman's teaching that you should probably ask an Elder for. But for now I can explain it to you a little. Women are the most powerful when they are on their moon time. Our bodies are completely in sync with the earth and water, with the moon cycles. The moon controls the tide, and that's why women are also keepers of the water. It's a time of rejuvenation for women, a time for healing. It's a time for us to release emotions and give them back to the earth. But usually women do this alone. Men have the same sort of thing with the sweat lodge and singing. Their breath and their song gives their pain back to the earth. The sweat lodge is a man's time for healing. Some women don't go into sweat lodges because they feel it's a man's place. But everywhere is different. Everyone has their own teachings. Each nation has a teaching that may be a little different from the next."

"How do you know all of this?" The lump in River's throat was back.

"I learned most of it when I had my berry fast. When I was first becoming a woman." She looked at River to see if she understood. "Going through puberty," she added.

"What's a berry fast?" River asked.

"A berry fast is a time you spend with the women you are closest to, maybe your nokomis. They teach you what it means to be a woman in the context of our culture. Why don't you come back to the Elders Tea this weekend? You can sit and mingle with Elders over tea and cookies. And you can ask them questions."

"Really?" The lump in River's throat dissolved at the idea she could go and ask questions and not feel stupid. "That sounds exactly like what I need."

"Yeah, us too," agreed Stephanie. When Brianna glared at her, she changed it to, "Um, me too."

"Great! We started the tea with the school kids to connect them with the Elders. The Elders loved it so much, they opened it up to the community. Many of them are lonely, and it helps keep them social. And it keeps our culture alive. So it's definitely a win-win."

"That sounds beautiful," River offered.

"It really is," Jennifer said with a smile, as she handed each girl a ribbon skirt, a shirt and a towel. "Get changed. Then we'll go out to the back and see if the Grandfather rocks are ready."

River had no idea what that meant, but she felt bad that she was holding them up with things she felt she ought to know. She changed and followed Jennifer out to the back of the building. The wigwam-looking lodge out there was made of willow branches and covered in layered deer hides. The scent of burning cedar and smudge lingered in the air. A young man in baggy pants and a white T-shirt poked the fire a little to move the rocks around. River counted seven rocks glowing red in the middle of the fire pit.

Jennifer handed the girls a small copper bowl and some small cedar branches. "Clean the cedar from the branch stem, by peeling it like this." Jennifer showed them, placing the cedar bits in the bowl. "We use this in the water we will be pouring over the rocks inside the lodge."

River listened, not saying a word. She peeled the cedar carefully. Her body tingled.

"When you are ready," Jennifer went on, "have a drink of water before you come in. When you open the door and crawl in, crawl in to your left."

River pulled her skirt up to her knees. Kneeling before the doorway of the lodge, she paused to take in everything she was doing. She pulled the warm leather hides to the side and crawled in to her left. Her lungs filled with warm air. It was kind of like a sauna, but even moister. Cedar branches covered the floor of the lodge. As she sat, she felt with her bare feet that the earth was cool beneath her. She dug in her toes. She wrapped her arms around her knees and closed her eyes. Her body relaxed. Her mind was at ease. She had no idea what to expect, but she did know one thing for certain. Being there felt right.

The young man keeping the fire closed the leather door after Jennifer climbed in. She shook her rattle. River remembered her nokomis's story that the sound of the rattle was the first sound man ever heard on earth. She didn't know the whole teaching, but she knew the rattle was a beautiful sound. Jennifer started singing. The song was like nothing River had ever heard before. Jennifer invited the glowing red rocks into the middle of the lodge and poured cedar water over them.

As the steam filled River's lungs, she started to weep. It wasn't from the heat. It was from the overwhelming sense of love, pain and joy that flowed into her along with the steam. River had no idea where the feeling came from or what it meant. But in the moment she didn't care. It filled her up. It felt good. It felt right.

August 13

There are no words.

There are no words to describe this feeling. This sense of relief.

I usually have no problem thinking of things to journal about. But all I can think about right now is how amazing it felt to be in the presence of Jennifer. Listening to her speak about what she has been taught about our culture. I wish I could be just like her. She is stunning, kind, funny, smart. And she rocks her beadwork.

And she introduced me to the sweat lodge. It was the most amazing thing I have ever done. The feeling you have inside is indescribable, and not just because you can barely breathe! It feels like home.

Is it weird to say I felt beautiful in the ribbon skirt?

Speaking of feeling beautiful, it was weird to see Russell after the circle. I could tell we both knew that we weren't interested in each other anymore, if we ever were. I thought I wanted to be a different person, and being with Russell made that easy. But I don't really want to be that person. And I don't want to get close to Russell until I figure out who I really am.

I'm not who I used to be with Josh, either. I have to have a hard conversation with him. I can feel that I have already grown beyond my relationship with him. I need more. I want more. And not from him. It's nothing he can give me.

And finally, I need Mom to know that I am okay with what happens next. I had a very different life from the kids here. I know that my childhood has been a good one. Not perfect, but good. And having her protect and nurture me my whole life gave me a chance to find my way out of the shit storm that could have happened here.

I realize that this is the first time in a long time I have felt like myself, just me. Not a farm girl, not a daughter, or a girlfriend, or a friend. Just me.

CHAPTER 27

Grandmother is Kind

"Okay, awesome, Mom, I'll see you in a couple weeks. I love you too." River put her phone in her pocket and walked back into the house. The whole place smelled of bannock.

Her nokomis poured icing sugar into a tiny bowl. She set jam, honey, butter and a knife on the table. "Pick your evil," she said. "Mine's honey. A long time ago we would just dip it in lard."

"Mmm, did you make piggy rolls too?" River said, wiggling her eyebrows.

"What on heaven's earth are piggy rolls?" her nokomis asked with a grin. "Or do I want to even know?"

"Ever dirty, Noki!" River laughed. "They're just hot dog wieners rolled in scone dough and then deep-fried."

"Oh, yum! I love wieners!"

"Nokomis!" River groaned. She loved her noki's sense of humour. She couldn't wait until she was old enough to get away with saying things like that.

Eric walked into the kitchen. "Mmmm. Smells good, Mom."

River and her nokomis looked at each other and burst into laughter.

"What?" Eric looked puzzled.

"Get washed up for lunch, Eric. We're having bannock with our soup today."

"Okay, Mother." Eric's tone was sarcastic. But his kiss on her cheek was warm.

Grace continued. "So, my girl, how do you feel about the healing circle and sweat lodge? I didn't want to ask right after. Sometimes you need quiet time after a day like that."

"Well . . ." River smiled nervously. She placed her palm under her chin. "It was really good. I think it's exactly what everyone needed. It felt good to be there. Before that, all I felt was anger at those girls." River paused, and then went on. "I realized a few things. Like how disconnected from my culture, and from myself, I am. I don't know any of the teachings. So I felt kind of stupid a few times."

Her nokomis interrupted. "Oh, my girl, don't feel like that at all. Everyone is on a different path, and in a different place within that learning journey. You're not judged by how many or how few teachings you know."

"I know . . . I just — I wish I knew more. But there's an Elders Tea that I'd like to go to."

"Oh yes, I go to that once a month too. I find every week is too much for me. I guess I like my alone time too much."

"The sweat lodge was incredible, Noki. I felt really grounded, literally half naked on the earth. It was surreal."

Her nokomis said nothing. But she had her all-knowing grin stretching from ear to ear.

"Uh . . . I learned a little more about moon time and stuff," said River. "And some new songs in the lodge."

Grace nodded.

"I learned that if you put your mouth close to the ground, you can get some relief from the heat. The earth is so cool."

Grace nodded a second time.

"And the strangest thing, Noki, was the feeling I had. I can't really describe it. It just felt like . . . home. Does that make any sense?"

Her nokomis's eyes were as gentle as the bunnies back on the farm as she said, "It makes perfect sense. When you are connected to the earth, you are close to creation, and connected to your own spirit. You can live in a bunch of different places in the world, River, and you may never call any of them home. The true meaning of home is not your physical place in the world. It's where you fit in the order of creation. You are part of the earth. You are not separate from it. That's why physical things don't really bring people much happiness at all. True happiness comes from the love you feel from the earth and creation."

"Whatever it is, it feels amazing."

"It certainly does, my girl. It certainly does." Her nokomis paused, and then asked, "And now that you are finding your home, are you ready to talk about your 'stuff' back home, my girl?"

Eric returned from washing his hands. "I haven't wanted to upset you, Riv. But can I ask what's going on with your mom and you?"

"I know. Sorry, guys. I was really trying to forget about it all. And then with everything that has happened here, I feel like I'm this huge burden to everyone. I didn't want to bring up more drama." River's eyes were on the floor.

"It's okay, my girl, we are both here for you," Eric said.

"Well, Randy is the reason she's leaving. He is so abusive, Dad. Verbally and emotionally. He's not really abusive to me, but I watch a lot of it happen to Mom. He screams and has tantrums like a toddler. He smashes dishes. He's always mad at me, or about me. And he's just friggin' creepy sometimes when my friends are over."

"Geez, River. You know, growing up witnessing violence is just as bad as being abused directly. It still affects you whether you realize it or not," Eric warned.

"Yeah," River said, nodding. "I guess I never really thought of it that way. But, Dad, I'm okay. Really okay. Listening to the others at the youth circle every week, and at the healing circle, kind of forced me to get some perspective. There are young people who are just trying to make it through the day facing whatever horrible challenge it is they have to face. Some kids don't have a high school in their community so they have to go live with strangers. No wonder they end up in gangs! Some kids live in so much poverty that their main concern is feeding their siblings. It made me realize how privileged I am. I have lived a good life. Now I feel like my move to the rez will be less overwhelming, because I know that I'll be with Mom, and I'll be safe."

Eric and Grace smiled at each other and then at River. "Sounds like you have grown a little in the last few weeks, Riv," Eric said proudly.

"I guess so," River responded.

"For the record," Eric said to River, "I'm sorry you had to go through all this. Just because it may not feel as bad as what others are going through, it can still be tough. You can still ask for help in dealing with stuff. Because before you know it, these little things can become lots of little things, which can then become big problems. Don't hold anything in, my girl."

"I know, Dad. Thank you. I journal, you know, as an easier way for me to express myself. Even if it's just *to* myself."

"That's really wonderful to hear, River," her nokomis offered. "You know, journaling is like storytelling, and so is art. Our ancestors have expressed themselves for centuries through storytelling. It's how our culture survived. Indigenous women used to pass the time telling stories, and pass on traditions through art. I think my favourite traditional art is basket making with birch bark. You should come harvesting with me before you go back home."

"Aww, Noki, what am I going to do without you around all the time?!" whined River. "I learn so much from you every single day. I would love to go harvesting with you." River sneaked a peek at her cell phone. "What about in the morning, Noki? It's supposed to be sunny all day tomorrow. Low winds and no chance of rain."

"How do you know that, River?" Eric asked.

She held up her phone. "I looked it up on the inter-web," she teased.

As they all laughed, her nokomis said, "It's a date, my girl!"

CHAPTER 28

They Gather Birch Bark

The birds were already "praying" by four a.m. River groaned. She rolled over and pulled the sheets above her head. She knew this was going to be one of her last days with her nokomis that summer, so she didn't want it to even start.

An hour later, River crawled out of bed and decided to make everyone omelettes for breakfast. She packed a lunch for herself and her nokomis, and gathered the bug spray, a blanket and a hat. She looked at her red bandana but let it rest on the dresser.

Grace made her way slowly down the stairs and gathered a few things before she sat down for breakfast. "Good morning, my girl. You're up awfully early. Breakfast smells delicious. Thank you."

"You're welcome, Nokomis." River smiled as she poured some coffee.

Grace stirred a sugar cube into her cup. "We will need to drive for about an hour north to this one special area. It's an old logging road, so no one will be around on the weekend."

"Awesome. I grabbed us everything we need. As soon as you're ready, let me know."

"Great. Don't forget your bundle."

They finished their breakfast, hopped in the car and drove

toward the sun until they turned north. When they arrived at the logging road, River put the car into park and helped Grace gather her satchel and bundle. Grace placed her bundle on the ground and laid the red cloth out flat. She had two little white tobacco ties — natural tobacco leaves crumbled into a little piece of cloth with a leather tie around it. She had her smudge bowl, her feather and her other medicines in leather pouches. She handed a tobacco tie to River.

"We offer this tobacco, this semaa, to introduce ourselves to the Creator." They placed the tobacco on the ground under the tree. River now knew it was to give thanks for the gift from the earth they were about to receive. "We take only what we need," Grace reminded River.

Grace pulled her bush knife from its leather sheath. The handle was carved from deer antler with a tiny image of a wolf by artist Norman Knott. She held the knife to the bark of the birch tree and sliced horizontally around the tree trunk about a foot above her head. Three feet down, she made another horizontal slice all the way around the tree. She then made a final vertical slice from the top cut to the bottom cut. She poked the knife into the layers of bark, almost as if she were filleting a fish, separating the flesh from the bones. River could see the layers revealing themselves until Grace finally made it to the light-colored, wet centre of the tree.

"Avoid cutting the inside of the tree, so you don't damage it. Only the outer bark is harvested, so the tree can continue to grow. Here, you try." Grace handed River the knife.

River stepped up to a tree, laid town her semaa tie and started praying. She paused and looked up at her nokomis. "I think I need a spirit name, Nokomis. Maybe it would help me when I introduce myself to the Creator?"

"I think that's an excellent idea, my girl."

River sliced the bark, exactly as her nokomis had shown. First the top cut. Then the bottom cut. Then the vertical slice. She had a tricky time finding the inner white layer of the tree. She was nervous she would damage it and wasn't pressing very hard.

"It's good to practise on these trees on the logging road, River. They will be cut down, so you won't damage a tree that needs to live. Don't be nervous, you'll find the inner layer," her nokomis reassured her.

River wiggled the knife until she was able to peel the bark from around the tree. She felt absolutely elated. She felt like she was glowing.

River fell to her knees and burst into tears. Grace placed a warm hand on her back. She pulled sage and her smudge bowl from her bundle. She lit the sage with a match and offered the bowl to River. River smudged, kneeling beneath the birch trees. Then she sat down with the bark and knife at her feet. She looked up at her nokomis and asked, "This is what home feels like, isn't it, Noki?"

"Yes, my girl, yes. This is exactly what home feels like."

"Thank you, Nokomis, for bringing me here." River sniffled. "It doesn't matter where I live, just like you said. I get it now. It really is about my connection to the earth and to the Creator. Finding and listening to my spirit is what's going to help me find my way through life, isn't it?"

"You got it, my girl."

Grace gathered her bundle and held her hand out to River. River pulled herself up into her nokomis's arms and hugged her tight.

"Here, let's sit over here," said Grace. "Maybe we'll have a snack or something. I'm hungry already, and I have another story to tell you."

River and her nokomis settled in on their blanket under a large willow tree. Grace nibbled on a sandwich while River collected herself. And then she started the story.

"You know, long ago, when women had babies, they kept them in a piece of wood called a cradleboard. The babies were swaddled in a blanket or cloth, or probably deer hide way back when, and then secured to the cradleboard. Then mothers carried their babies on their backs or hung them in or on their lodging, or even in a tree. This kept the babies safe and happy while the mothers worked. They kept a moss bag for the baby, before cloth diapers came around."

River smiled and found a more comfortable position on the blanket.

"The Elders also used to say that the teaching in the cradleboard is the first teaching a baby receives. The baby learns to watch, observe and listen. The baby pays very close attention to the things going on around him or her. Babies learn to observe before they learn to speak. And some people even say this is why our people are so quiet sometimes even now. Even politicians, or people in the public eye. We have always listened and observed since we were infants. We thought about things before we made decisions, or before we spoke up. Sometimes people talk so much, they don't spend any time listening. People who talk a lot aren't truly listening. And you can't learn much if you aren't listening, if you're doing all the talking."

"I know the type," River groaned. "That makes perfect sense."

"You said you want your spirit name, River."

"Yes," replied River. "I realize I want to be able to introduce myself with a spirit name, in Anishnaabomowin. Like you do."

"Well, that's something that you could ask an Elder for. You prepare some semaa and you offer it to an Elder you are close with. If they accept it from you, that means they will want to talk with you and get to know you better. They will wait until the name comes to them. Sometimes it comes to them in a dream, or a vision. When they are ready, they will let you know to come and visit them. You can have a naming ceremony at that time. They will introduce you to the people and to the Creator using your spirit name. Then you have a little giveaway, kind of like party favours. You make special things to give away, to thank the people who came to support you. It's like the opposite of a birthday party where you get things. This is more like a gratitude party where you give things, to thank the people for coming."

"Is that why they have giveaways at the end of the powwow, to thank the dancers and singers for coming?"

"Exactly, my girl."

"Cool," River mused. "So if you have a spirit name, why do you only say it in our language, and not in English?"

"Well, some people believe the name is only between you and the Creator, so they don't share it with anyone, or anyone who is not very close to you. Most people don't translate into English because the meaning gets lost. Native languages are so descriptive that the English version would be too long a name to call someone. Take my name for example. In Anishnaabomowin, my name means, *the moment the lightning from the thunderbird's eyes hits the ground.* There is no word for that particular moment, so you have to describe it. And to describe it would take forever in Ojibwe, so they call me *Nimke Biiniishe Kwe*, which simply translates to *Thunder Bird Woman*. When I introduce myself to speakers of the language I explain my whole name, though. This is why it is so important to learn and preserve our language. So we can maintain our culture."

"Nokomis, you have so much knowledge. I want to listen to your stories and teachings forever." River played with some blades of grass. She knew if she met her nokomis's eye, she would burst into tears again.

"Well, I'm only a phone call away, my girl. And you are always welcome here anytime too. You can even bring a friend next time if you like. Your old noki has lots of stories, remember?" She winked.

"Yeah, that would be fun. But I don't want to share you with anyone," River giggled.

"You feel ready to go harvest some more bark? My belly is full, and so is my heart."

"Yes, Noki, let's do this." River hopped up, tidied her space and helped her nokomis up off the ground. She grabbed her knife in its sheath and let her nokomis lead the way.

Together, River and her nokomis harvested until they couldn't stand the mosquitos anymore. It was almost dusk when they slammed the door of the car trunk, full of birch bark scrolls.

Grace looked up at River. "Miigwech for today, River. After I show you how to clean the bark, I'm going to show you how to bite it."

"Bite it?" Was she joking?

"Yeah, bite it. It's called birch bark biting. It's a really old art form. Mostly women used to do it to pass the time, or to decorate baskets. They used an eye tooth to make floral patterns, animals, insects — anything in nature."

"Nokomis, that sounds amazing!"

"I like to use my front teeth. My eye teeth are so far back in my mouth that I can't use them. So my birch bark biting always looks a little different from anyone else's," Grace explained.

"Oh, so you're talented *and* unique, eh?" River teased.

"Unique is an understatement, my girl," Grace laughed. "And speaking of talented, I'd like to go to bingo tomorrow. Do you want to come with me?"

"Ha! I'd love to, Noki."

August 24

Watching Noki at bingo is a riot! I can't keep up with her!

I have had a huge awakening, spending time with my nokomis. She has taught me about the land and being a strong Indigenous woman. I wish there had been someone in my life to help me with a berry fast when I was becoming a woman. Maybe it wouldn't have felt like such a terrible curse. Mom just gave me pads, like, "Here are some pads. You're gonna get your period. Take some ibuprofen. Basically, it sucks."

Which is true.

When I think about my nokomis and everything she has taught me in such a short time, it makes me feel weepy. That's partly because I know she's not going to be around forever. I am so thankful she gave me this Anishnaabomowin book. I have so much more to learn from her. Maybe I should stay here with her. Who is going to listen to all her stories and make sure they are passed on to the next generation of women? What if I move back home, and Noki doesn't make it to next summer when I come back?

And it's not like I even know what home is going to look like or be like. But I'm not scared of going home anymore, even with the uncertainty. I know I can handle whatever is waiting for me.

The first thing I'm going to have to tell Mom is that I got beat up. She's going to freak because I didn't tell her sooner. Honestly, I just wanted to put it all behind me. But I know I need to tell her the complete truth, so we can start a new sort of relationship. One of honesty. I want her to know how much I do love her, and that I am thankful she is my mom. She has always been by my side. If there's one thing I have learned this summer, it's that that's what good parents do.

And now I'm weeping again. Dad probably doesn't notice because he's singing along to the radio, playing his air guitar.

I'll be happy to see Mom.

I'll be happy to sleep in my own bed. I miss my pillow. I totally should have brought it with me.

I guess that's it for now. I have to pack up and say my goodbyes.

GIIWEBZON

CHAPTER 29

Drive Home

"You know, Dad, I had no idea what to expect this summer. And I have to say, it didn't turn out at all like what I imagined." River had her arms wrapped tightly around Eric's neck.

Eric stood back and held his daughter's hands in his. "Me too, Riv, me too. I wasn't sure how it was going to be this summer, especially with your sudden departure from your mom's. And your staying three times as long as we had planned. But I really feel happy that you were here with us, and that you got to spend some quality time with your nokomis."

At the mention of her grandmother, River walked over to where her nokomis was standing on the curb. River stepped down from the curb, so Grace stood at eye level with her. River took her hands in hers.

"Nokomis. Thank you for helping me this summer. I don't think I would have made it through without you."

"You are strong, my girl. Of course you would have. I'm just so glad I'm still here to see you grow up."

"Noki, I'm going to miss you sooo much! Can I come back for a visit at Christmas break?"

"Of course you can, my dear. We will be here, ready and waiting with the tea and bannock on. Ooh, and it will be winter time.

That would be so nice, since winter time is the best time for storytelling. I didn't get to tell you all my juicy stories this summer, since we got a little sidetracked." She winked.

"I know, Nokomis. I'm so sorry if I caused you any stress. I thought I was leaving it all behind me."

"And now you know that, wherever you go, it always catches up with you. That's why you have to deal with it, eh?" She held River's cheeks in the palms of her hands and kissed her on the forehead. "Don't forget to keep reading that Anishnaabomowin book. Practise the language a little each day. Before you know it, you will be having a conversation with me in Ojibwe."

"Mmm . . . that might be wishful thinking, Noki. I don't think it will happen that fast. I'm not that smart! But I must say, this is the best going-away-to-university present a girl could hope for."

"You are going to do so well, my girl." Her nokomis smiled as she tucked a hundred dollar bill into River's hand. "Shh, here's some zhoonia for you. Buy something nice for school."

"Zhoonia. Does that mean money?"

"Shhh, I said. Yes." She winked again.

"Okay . . . Miigwech, Nokomis," River whispered.

River turned to her dad once more. "Thanks again, Dad, for everything. I'll talk to you the first week of school, okay?"

"Okay," said Eric. "Well, text me when you get home. And text me if you need anything. And text me how it's going on the first day of classes."

"Eric," said Grace. "She's not going to text you all those times. Leave the poor girl alone." She looked at River with a serious face. "But text me. Okay, my girl?"

River smiled as she threw her backpack over her shoulder and made her way to the bus platform. She waved them goodbye.

* * *

Twenty-eight hours later, River was wrapping her arms around her mom's neck. She did not let go, even as her mother tried to pull away several times.

Her mom giggled, "I missed you too, River."

"You have no idea how much I missed you, Mom," River mumbled in her ear.

River's mom kissed her again on the forehead. "C'mon, let's get your bags. Are you hungry? You must be hungry. Are you tired? Oh, and Thomas is here, waiting to meet you."

River had a sinking feeling in her stomach. She thought she felt the lump in her throat surface again. "Yeah, I could use a bite to eat. Like a salad or something real."

River's mom took her hand. "Okay, we'll stop on the way home."

They walked toward a man standing and scrolling through his phone. River was trying to smile with her eyes, but she thought it might look like she was going to be sick.

"River, this is Thomas," said her mom formally. "Thomas, River." Her smile was wide, uncertain.

"Hey." River stuck out her hand to shake.

"Ahniin, River. Nice to finally meet you," Thomas replied. His voice was gentle and his body language soft. River was surprised. She was expecting a stoic Native man with a deep voice and a firm handshake.

"You too," she managed.

River and her mom linked arms as Thomas grabbed River's large backpack and trailed behind them. "So tell me everything, Riv. How was your summer at your dad's?"

River winced. "It's kind of a long story, Mom. Can we talk about it later?"

"Oh yes, of course. You must be tired from travelling. Let me take you to the café on the rez. They have the most amazing Indian tacos, and the best bannock you have ever tasted."

"Umm, I don't know about that, Mom. My nokomis makes a pretty mean bannock."

"Mmm, bannock," Thomas squealed.

River was surprised to find herself laughing along with her mom and this new man.

"Okay, I'll try it, Mom," agreed River.

They hopped into the car and made their way home. River's tummy was in knots during the entire ride. She wondered what her new room would look like. She wondered if Thomas's kids would like her. She wondered what university was going to be like. She gazed out the window and didn't listen to a word they said in the front seats.

She drifted into thinking about the conversations she needed to have with her family and friends in Ontario. Normally, something like that would make her anxious. But she felt in her heart that this time, everything really was going to be okay.

NGII-MNO-MAAJAAMI

CHAPTER 30

We Left in a Good Way

River noticed a difference between this reserve and the one in Winnipeg. The houses weren't quite as shabby. There weren't fifteen hundred smoke shops on the way in. Just one, with a fairly new-looking gas station and convenience store. They came to the only four-way stop with a flashing light. There was a quaint little art gallery, and Thomas explained to River that the owners were the first Indigenous millionaires in Canada. They passed a small school with a beautiful sign that looked like it was painted by the kids. River thought about her elementary school days. She thought about Charlie and Jazz, her best friends from those days, and how she had neglected them in the last couple of months.

"Oh, I have a cool story for you, River, about your new home." Thomas looked in the rear-view mirror to meet her eyes.

River remained silent but listened respectfully.

"We rent Elsie Knott's house. She was the first woman chief ever in Canada. Her daughter Rita was the Anishnaabomowin teacher at our elementary school for the longest time, but I think she's retired now. Anyway, Elsie did a lot of amazing things for the community. She drove the kids to school every day in the next town. She even bought a hearse with her own money, because there was more room in it to cart the kids to school. She raised funds for things like building the church and the school. It's too bad that so few people know her story. She was a band-council chief, which is different from our traditional ways of governance. But she did an amazing job despite all the barriers she had to work through."

"That's really cool, Thomas," River piped up from behind him. "I was learning about that kind of stuff this summer, treaties and band councils."

"What treaty area is your dad from, River?"

"Oh, Treaty One. We still get five bucks a year."

Thomas laughed. "Good old treaty money, not accounting for inflation!"

"Right?!" River laughed.

River saw her mother smile, and was happy to know that she and Thomas getting along caused it.

"We're Williams Treaty here," said Thomas. "Have you heard about the big settlement in this area?"

"No, I haven't," River responded.

"Oh, then we have lots to talk about." This time Thomas looked over his shoulder to smile at River.

River smiled back politely, and felt the walls she had set up slowly recede. *Maybe Thomas isn't going to be so bad after all*, she thought.

"I can also introduce you to some people your age if you want to get involved in the community. I don't know if your mom told you or not. I'm the guidance counselor at the high school, and the youth coordinator here on the rez."

"Oh, no I don't think she did tell me." She shot her mom a look that said, *Why did you keep that awesome news from me?* Her mom made a face at her. "So what's it like there?" River inquired.

"What do you mean?" asked Thomas.

"The other kids, what are they like?"

"Just like any other kids, I guess. They walk around in headphones, they talk back, they fall asleep in class. Just like nonnative kids."

River giggled. "I guess I meant are any of the youth into culture. Are there any cultural activities to do here?"

"Oh yes, I see," said Thomas. "Yes, totally. There's a big drum social once a month, and the youth host it. There's a beading class at the library on Tuesday nights."

River interrupted, "That's awesome."

Thomas smiled and continued. "The health centre and library usually have cultural workshops once a month. Every month they do something different. For example, last month they did a two-day moose hair tufting workshop."

"Do they do birch bark biting here?" River asked, excitement entering her voice.

"Oh, I wish they did, River. That's such a rare thing these days. Not many people do it anymore."

"I know, right? I'm so lucky my nokomis taught me how to do that this summer."

Her mom smiled when Thomas exclaimed, "Really? Maybe you can show the others how to do it?"

"Umm . . . maybe. I would still feel kinda shy," River replied.

"All in time, my girl," Thomas said.

River felt that lump start up in her throat again. She hadn't expected for Thomas to call her, "my girl" so soon, if at all. He didn't seem to notice that he did it, so she let it slide. But she knew it was something she might be thinking about for the next while. Her relationship with her mom was everything. And so her relationship with Thomas was important to her mom. River was surprised to realize how much she wanted it to be good. She wanted Thomas to like her.

They pulled into a driveway, and the first thing River noticed was that the house was built of beautiful logs, with a gorgeous front porch. She saw a hammock and a chair swing, and what seemed to be a lending library in a makeshift china cabinet.

River thought, *This is not what I imagined.*

Thomas carried in her bags. River's mom sat down in the chair swing and gestured for River to lie in the hammock. "Wanna unwind a bit with me?"

"Sure, Mom." River hopped into the hammock. "Thomas is way different than I expected, Mom. He seems really nice."

"He really is, River. He's really such a beautiful soul."

"The house is not what I imagined, though. I thought it would be like the old rundown houses on the rez you usually see."

"Yeah, not everyone lives like that anymore. Times have changed a little. It's a little different in southern Ontario compared to more remote communities. It's not as hard and expensive to access good building materials here."

"True," River agreed.

"One thing, though. Thomas's kids just walk in and out of the house without knocking. And they come and borrow stuff when we're not here, like sugar or coffee. That's kinda weird, no?"

"Well, people share everything on the rez, Mom. That's just how it is, especially with immediate family. Heck, people share the craziest of things with strangers!"

River's mom shifted her body weight in the swing. "You know, River, I can't help but notice you've changed."

"What?" River laughed. "What do you mean? I'm the same old gal. I just had a few new experiences."

"Well whatever these experiences were, I see a definite shift. All good of course. You just seem . . . so *different.*"

"I guess I am a bit different after the summer I've had, Mom.

It's too much to get into right now. It's like I need a vacation from my vacation. But I guess you have had quite the month too, eh? We have a lot of catching up to do."

"Yes, sweetie, we do. We certainly do."

Thomas came out onto the front porch with a tray of glasses. A large dark cloud shaded the porch and birch trees, and thunder rolled through the sky. "Oh, the thunderbirds are out playing. Iced tea, anyone?"

He set the tray down and handed River and her mom their drinks. Then he raised his glass.

"Cheers to a new beginning!" he said. They clinked glasses. Thomas looked River straight in the eye and, to her delight, slurped his drink as loud as he could.

BAAMAAPII GAWAABMIN

EPILOGUE
See You Later

Before putting it away, I flipped through this journal that contains this story of mine. The story of my powwow summer. I'm starting university. I want to be at peace about the decisions I have made so I can move into the future.

It only took one summer to open my eyes to another world. I've decided it's a world I want to explore. I want to travel. I want to learn. I want to dance. I want to powwow all summer long, right across the country. Road trips every weekend. But no more 49s for a while.

I've decided I'll spend more time being in touch with my nokomis, and learning from the Elders. I have so much to learn before they're gone.

I have decided that Josh and I can be friends. Jazz is still in high school, and Charlie was off to another school anyway. Turns out, sometimes you outgrow friends. It doesn't mean you love them less. It just means that you take different paths. Mom said sometimes you stay friends forever. When you see each other in ten years, it's like you just saw them last week and you pick up right where you left off. I hope that Josh and Charlie and Jazz are still waiting for me then.

The best part of my summer I didn't even write about in my journal. It was getting my spirit name from my nokomis. I learned in the sweat lodge that some things are just meant to be left unsaid, and some things are meant to be sacred. That's why we don't record things like ceremonial songs and the act of ceremony itself.

But I remember the moment Eleanor, Nokomis's cousin, walked into the room in her beautiful red ribbon skirt. She sat beside my nokomis, laughing a huge gut laugh. It reminded me that they were young women once too, and that they never left their playful spirit behind. Nokomis giving me my spirit name in the presence of our community changed my life. Forever. I'm not that scared and wounded grade five girl being teased in the school yard. I am not that girl who ran to Winnipeg at the idea of moving to the reserve. It doesn't matter where I live, or who I am with, or who my friends are. I know who I am. I know that the Creator doesn't give us things we can't handle in life.

Adulting is hard. Paying for my own way through university is bittersweet too. I know that we have a right to education, because of the treaties. But I'm not living on my reserve, and I get that kids there should get first priority. Mom also reminded me that sometimes when you have to work harder for things, you end up appreciating them more. But I already know that taking Indigenous Studies is right for me, at least right now. And not just to learn more about myself and who I am. Once I get that figured out, I can find a way to make things better. I probably won't go into politics or anything, but this summer made me sure that, somehow, I want to help.

Nokomis told me that everything happens for a reason. Spirit lights the way, and it's up to me to watch and listen, just like in the cradleboard teaching. Nokomis also taught me to never say goodbye. It's always just 'see you later.' In Anishnaabomowin, it's simply Baamaapii, until we see each other again.

Baamaapi,

Gii-bmkaan-waanizhaad.

"She finds her way."

Seems like the perfect spirit name for me <3